UNLOCKING
THE AIR

and Other Stories

UNLOCKING THE AIR

and Other Stories

URSULA K. LE GUIN

HarperCollins*Publishers*

HarperCollins books may be purchased for educational, business, or sales promotional use. For information please write: Special Markets Department, HarperCollins Publishers, Inc., 10 East 53rd Street, New York, NY 10022.

FIRST EDITION

Designed by Caitlin Daniels

Library of Congress Cataloging-in-Publication Data
Le Guin, Ursula K., 1929–
   Unlocking the air and other stories / Ursula K. Le Guin.—1st ed.
    p. cm.
   ISBN 0-06-017260-6
   1. Manners and customs—Fiction. 2. Fantastic fiction, American.
I. Title.
PS3562.E42U56   1996
813'.54—dc20   95-36012

96 97 98 99 00 ❖/HC 10 9 8 7 6 5 4 3 2

ACKNOWLEDGMENTS

"Half Past Four," copyright © 1987 by Ursula K. Le Guin; first appeared in *The New Yorker.*

"The Professor's Houses," copyright © 1982 by Ursula K. Le Guin; first appeared in *The New Yorker.*

"Ruby on the 67," copyright © 1996 by Ursula K. Le Guin.

"Limberlost," copyright © 1989 by Ursula K. Le Guin; first appeared in *Michigan Review Quarterly.*

"The Creatures on My Mind," copyright © 1990 by Ursula K. Le Guin; first appeared in *Harper's.*

"Standing Ground," copyright © 1992 by Ursula K. Le Guin; first appeared in *Ms.*

"The Spoons in the Basement," copyright © 1982 by Ursula K. Le Guin; first appeared in *The New Yorker.*

"Sunday in Summer in Seatown," copyright © 1995 by Ursula K. Le Guin; first appeared in *13th Moon.*

"In the Drought," copyright © 1993 by Ursula K. Le Guin; first appeared in *Xanadu II.*

"Ether, OR," copyright © 1995 by Ursula K. Le Guin; first appeared in *Asimov's.*

"Unlocking the Air," copyright © 1990 by Ursula K. Le Guin; first appeared in *Playboy.*

"A Child Bride," copyright © 1987 by Ursula K. Le Guin; first appeared in *Terry's Universe* under the title "Kore 87."

"Climbing to the Moon," copyright © 1992 by Ursula K. Le Guin; first appeared in *American Short Fiction.*

"Daddy's Big Girl," copyright © 1987 by Ursula K. Le Guin; first appeared in *Omni.*

"Findings," copyright © 1992 by Ursula K. Le Guin; first appeared as a chapbook from Ox Head Press.

"Olders," copyright © 1995 by Ursula K. Le Guin; first appeared in *Omni.*

"The Wise Woman," copyright © 1995 by Ursula K. Le Guin; first broadcast on *The Sound of Writing.*

"The Poacher," copyright © 1992 by Ursula K. Le Guin; first appeared in *Xanadu.*

CONTENTS

UNLOCKING
THE AIR

and Other Stories

HALF PAST FOUR

A NEW LIFE

Stephen blushed. A fair-skinned man, bald to the crown, he blushed clear pink. He hugged Ann with one arm as she kissed his cheek. "Good to see you, honey," he said, freeing himself, glancing past her, and smiling rather desperately. "Ella just went out. Just ten minutes ago. She had to take some typing over to Bill Hoby. Stay around till she gets back, she'd be real sorry to miss you."

"Sure," Ann said. "Mother's fine, she had this flu, but not as bad as some people. You all been OK?"

"Oh, yeah, sure. You want some coffee? Coke? Come on in." He stood aside and followed her through the small living room crowded with blond furniture to the kitchen where yellow metal slat blinds directed sunlight in molten strips onto the counters.

"Hey, it's hot," Ann said.

"Want some coffee? There's this cinnamon and mocha decaf that Ella and I drink a lot. It sure is. Glad it's Saturday. It's up here somewhere."

"I don't want anything."

"Coke?" He closed the cupboard, opened the refrigerator.

"Oh, sure, OK. Diet if you've got it."

She stood by the counter and watched him get the glass and the ice and the bottle, a plastic half-gallon of cola. She did not want to open doors in this kitchen as if prying, as if entitled, or to change the angle of the slat blinds, as she would have done at home, to shut the hot light out. He fixed her a tall red plastic glass of cola, and she drank off half of it. "Oh, yeah!" she said. "OK!"

"Come on outside."

"No ball game?"

"Been doing some gardening. With Toddie."

Ann had assumed that the boy was with his mother, or rather her imagination had linked him to his mother so that if Ella wasn't here Toddie wasn't here; now she felt betrayed.

Indicating where she should go but making her go first, as when he had brought her through the house, her father ushered her to the back-porch door, and stood aside and followed her as she went past the washer and dryer and the mop bucket and some brooms to the screen door and down the single cement step into the back yard.

He batted the screen door shut with one foot and stood beside her on a brick path, two bricklengths wide, that ran along dividing the flowerbeds under the house wall from the small, shrub-circled lawn. Two small iron chairs painted white, with rust stains where the paint had come off, faced each other across a matching table at one side of the grass plot. Beyond them Toddie crouched, turned away, near a big flowering abelia in the shade of the mirrorplant hedge that enclosed the garden.

Toddie was bigger than she had remembered, as broad-backed as a grown man.

"Hey, Toddie. Here's ah, here's Ann!" Stephen said. His fair, tanned face was still pink. Maybe he wasn't blushing, maybe it was the heat. In the enclosed garden the sunlight glaring from the white house wall burned on the skin like an open fire. Had he

2

been going to say, "your sister"? His voice was loud and jovial. Toddie did not respond in any way.

Ann looked around at the garden. It was an airless, grass-floored room with high green walls and a ceiling of brightness. Beautiful pale-colored poppies swayed by the hose rack, growing in clean, weeded dirt. She looked back at them, away from the stocky figure crouched in the shade across the lawn. She did not want to look at him, and her father had no right to make her be with him and look at him, even if it was superstitious, he should think of protecting the baby, but that was stupid, that was super-stitious. "Those are really neat," she said, touching the loose, soft petal of an open poppy. "Terrific colors. This is a nice garden, Daddy. You must have been working hard on it."

"Haven't you ever been out back here?"

She shook her head. She had never even been in the bed-rooms. She had been three or four times to this house since Stephen and Ella married. Once for Sunday brunch. Ella had served on trays in the living room, and Toddie had watched TV the whole time. The first time she had been in the house was when Ella was one of Stephen's salesgirls, not his wife. They had stopped by her house for her father to leave off some papers or something. Ann had been in high school, she had stood around in the living room while her father and Ella talked about shoe orders. Knowing that Ella had a retarded child, she had hoped that it wouldn't come into the room but all the same had wanted to see it. When Ella's husband died suddenly of something, Ann's father had said solemnly at the dinner table, "Lucky thing they had that house of theirs paid off," and Ann's mother had said, "Poor thing, with that poor child of theirs, what is it, a mon-goloid?" and then they had talked about how mongoloids usually died and it was a mercy. But here he was still alive and Stephen was living in his house.

"I need some shade," Ann said, heading for the iron chairs. "Come and talk with me, Daddy."

He followed her. While she sat down and slipped off her sandals to cool her bare feet in the grass, he stood there. She looked up at him. The curve of his bald forehead shone in the sunlight, open and noble as a high hill standing bare above a crowded subdivision. His face was suburban, crowded with features, chin and long lips and nostrils and fleshy nose and the small, clear, anxious blue eyes. Only the forehead that looked like a big California hill had room. "Oh, Daddy," she said, "how you *been*?"

"Just fine. Just fine," he said, half turned away from her. "The Walnut Creek store is going just great. Walking shoes." He bent to uproot a small dandelion from the short, coarse grass. "Walking shoes outsell running shoes two to one at the Mall. So, you been job hunting? You ever talk to Krim?"

"Oh, yeah, couple weeks ago." Ann yawned. The still heat and the smell of newly turned earth made her sleepy. Everything made her sleepy. Waking up made her sleepy. She yawned again. "Excuse me! He said, oh, he said something might would open up in May."

"Good. Good. Good outfit," Stephen said, looking around the garden, and moving a few steps away. "Good contacts."

"But I'll have to stop working in July because of the baby, so I don't know if it's worth it."

"Get to know people, get started," Stephen said indistinctly. He went to the edge of the lawn nearest the abelia and said in a cheerful, loud voice, "Hey, great work there, Toddie! Hey, look at that! That's my boy. All right!"

A blurred, whitish face under dark hair turned up to him for a moment in shadow.

"Look at that. Diggin' up a storm there. You're a real farmer." Stephen turned and spoke to Ann from shade across the white molten air to her strip of shade: "Toddie's going to put in some more flowers here. Bulbs and stuff for fall."

Ann drank her melted-ice water and got up from the dwarf chair that had already stained her white T-shirt with rust. She

came over nearer her father and looked at the strip of upturned earth. The big boy crouched motionless, trowel in hand, head sunk.

"Look, why not sort of round off that corner, see," Stephen said to him, going forward to point. "Dig to here, maybe. Think so?"

The boy nodded and began digging, slowly and forcefully. His hands were white and thick, with very short, wide nails rimmed with black dirt.

"What do you think, maybe dig it up clear over to that rose bush. Space out the bulbs better. Think it'd look good?"

Toddie looked up at him again. Ann looked at the blurred mouth, the dark-haired upper lip. "Yeah, uh-huh," Toddie said, and bent to work again.

"Kind of curve it off there at the rose bush," Stephen said. He glanced round at Ann. His face was relaxed, uncrowded. "This guy's a natural farmer," he said. "Get anything to grow. Teachin' me. Isn't that right, Toddie? Teachin' me!"

"I guess," the low voice said. The head stayed bowed, the thick fingers groped in earth.

Stephen smiled at Ann. "Teachin' me," he said.

"That's neat," she said. The sides of her mouth felt very stiff and her throat ached. "Listen, Daddy, I just looked in to say hi on the way to Permanente, I'm supposed to have a check-up. No, look, I'll just leave this in the kitchen and go out the gate there. It's real good to see you, Daddy."

"Got to go already," he said.

"Yeah, I just wanted to say hi since I was over this way. Say hi to Ella for me. I'm sorry I missed her." She had slipped her sandals back on; she took her empty glass into the kitchen, set it in the sink and ran water into it, came out again to her father standing on the brick path, bald to the sun. She put one foot up on the cement step to refasten the sandal. "My ankles were all swelled up," she said. "Dr. Schell took me off salt. I can't put salt on anything, not even eggs."

"Yeah, they say we should all cut down on salt," Stephen said.

"Yeah, that's right." After a pause Ann said, "Only this is because of being pregnant, that I have high blood pressure and this edema stuff. Unless I'm careful." She looked at her father. He was looking across the lawn.

"You know, Daddy, even if the baby doesn't have a father it can have a grandfather," she said. She laughed, and blushed, feeling the red heat mask her face and tingle in her scalp.

"Yeah, well, sure," he said, "I guess, you know," and if he finished the sentence she did not understand it. "We all got to take care," he said.

"Sure. Well, you take care too, Daddy," she said. She came to him to kiss his cheek. She tasted the faint salt of his sweat on her lips as she went along the brick path to the gate next to the trash cans, and let herself out onto the sidewalk under a purple jacaranda in full flower, and fastened the gate behind her.

UNBREAKING

"My back itches."

Ann reached out the garden fork and lightly raked its clawed tines down her brother's spine.

"Not there. There." He wrapped an arm round himself trying to show her the spot, his thick fingers with dirt-caked nails scrabbling in the air.

She hitched forward and scratched his back vigorously with her own fingertips. "That got it?"

"Uh-huh."

"I want some lemonade."

"Uh-huh," Todd said as she got up, whacking dirt off her bare knees. She had to bend at the knees, not at the waist, to reach them.

The yellow kitchen was hot and close like the inside of a room in a beehive, a cell full of yellow light, smelling of sweet

wax, airless. A grub would love it. Ann mixed up instant lemonade, poured it over ice in tall plastic glasses, and carried them out, kicking the screen door shut behind her.

"Here you go, Todd."

He straightened up kneeling and took the glass in his left hand without putting down the trowel in his right. He drank off half the lemonade and then stooped to dig again, still holding the glass.

"Put it down there," Ann said, "by the bush."

He put the glass down carefully on the weedy dirt, and went on digging.

"Hey that's good!" Ann said, sucking at her lemonade, her mouth squirting saliva like a lawn sprinkler. She sat down on the grass with her head in the shade and her legs in the sun, and chewed ice slowly.

"You aren't digging," Todd said after a while.

"Nope."

After a while she told him, "Drink your lemonade. The ice is all melting."

He put down the trowel and picked up the glass. After drinking the lemonade he put the empty glass where it had been before.

"Hey, Ann," he said, not digging, but kneeling there with his bare, thick, pale back to her.

"Hey, Todd."

"Is Daddy coming home at Christmas?"

She tried for a moment to figure this one out. She was too sleepy. "No," she said. "He isn't coming home at all. You know that."

"I thought at Christmas," her brother said, barely audible.

"At Christmas he'll be with his new wife, with Marie. That's where he lives now, that's where his home is, in Riverside."

"I thought he might visit. At Christmas."

"No. He won't do that."

Todd was silent. He picked up the trowel and laid it down again. Ann knew he was unsatisfied but she could not figure out what his problem was and did not want any problems. She got her back against the trunk of the camphor tree and sat feeling the sun on her legs and the prickling grass under them and a sweat-drop trickle down between her breasts and the baby move once softly deep in and over on the left side of the universe.

"Maybe we could ask him to come at Christmas," Todd said.

"Honey," Ann said, "we can't do that. He and Mama got divorced so he could marry Marie. Right? And he'll have Christmas with her now. With Marie. And we'll have our Christmas here like always. Right?" She waited for his nod. She was not sure she got one, but went on anyhow. "If you're missing him a lot, Todd, we can write him and tell him that."

"Maybe we could visit him."

Oh, yeah, dandy. Hi Daddy, here's your moron son and your unwed pregnant daughter on welfare, hi Marie! It struck her funny but not enough to laugh. "We can't," she said. "Hey, look. If you dig over to the end there, in front of the roses, we could put in those canna bulbs Mama got, too. They'd look real good there. They'll be red, big red lilies."

Todd picked up the trowel, and then laid it down again in the same place.

"After Christmas he has to come," he said.

"What for? Why does he have to?"

"For the baby," her brother said, very low and blurry.

"Oh," Ann said. "Oh, shit. OK. Well. Listen, Toddie. Look. I'm having the baby, right?"

"After Christmas."

"Right. And it will be mine. Ours. You and Mama are going to help me bring it up. Right? And that's all I need. All I want. All the baby wants. Just you and Mama. All right?" She waited for his nod. "You're going to help me with the baby. Tell me when it cries. Play with it. Like that little girl at school, Sandy, that you help with. OK, Toddie?"

"Yeah. Sure," her brother said in the voice he had sometimes, masculine and matter-of-fact, as if a man spoke through him from somewhere else. He knelt erect, his hands splayed on his bluejeaned thighs, his face and torso in shadow illuminated by the glare of sunlight on the grass. "But he's an older parent," he said.

He's an ex-parent, Ann stopped herself from saying. "Right. So what?"

"Older parents often have Down children."

"Older mothers do. Right. So?"

She looked at Todd's round, heavy face, the sparse mustache at the ends of the upper lip, the dark eyes. He looked away.

"So your baby could be a Down baby," he said.

"Sure, it could. But I'm not an older parent, honey."

"But Daddy is."

"Oh," Ann said, and after a pause, "Right." She hitched herself heavily into the shade, with her bare feet in the fresh dirt Todd had been digging up. "OK, listen, Todd. Daddy is your father. And my father. But *not* the *baby's* father. Right?" No nod. "The baby has a different father. You don't know the baby's father. He doesn't live here. He lives in Davis, where I was. And Daddy is—Daddy isn't anything. He isn't interested. He has a new family. A new wife. Maybe they'll have a baby. They can be older parents. But they can't have this baby. I'm having this baby. It's our baby. It doesn't *have* any father. It doesn't have any *grandfather*. It's got me and Mama and you. Right? You're going to be its uncle. Did you know that? Will you be the baby's Uncle Todd?"

"Yeah," Todd said unhappily. "Sure."

A couple of months ago when she was crying all the time she would have cried, but now the universe inside her surrounded her with distance, through which all emotions travelled so far to reach her that they became quiet and smooth, deep and soft, like the big unbreaking waves out in mid-ocean. Instead of crying she thought about crying, the salty ache. She picked up the three-tined garden fork and reached over, trying to scratch Todd's head with it. He had shifted out of reach.

"Hey kids," their mother said, the screen door banging behind her.

"Hey Ella," Ann said.

"Hi Mama," Todd said, turning away, bending to dig.

"Lemonade in the fridge," Ann said.

"What are you doing? Planting those old bulbs? I dug them up I don't know when, I bet they won't grow now. The cannas ought to. Oh I'm so hot! It's so hot downtown!" She came across the lawn in her high-heeled sandals, pantyhose, yellow cotton shirt dress, silk scarf, makeup, nail polish, sprayed set dyed hair, full secretarial uniform, complete armor. She bent over to kiss the top of her son's head, and kicked the sole of Ann's bare foot with the toe of her sandal. "Dirty children," she said. "Oh! It's so hot! I'm going to have a shower!" She went back across the lawn. The screen door banged. Ann imagined the soft folds released from under the girdle, the makeup sluiced away under warm spraying water running down over her first universe, that soft distance where she lived now, joined.

THE TIGER

Ella had on her yellow sleeveless dress with the black patent belt and black jet costume earrings. She had sprayed her hair. "Who's coming?" Ann asked from the couch.

"I told you yesterday. Stephen Sandies." Ella clipped past on her high wedge-heeled sandals like a circus pony on stilts, leaving a faint wake of hairspray smell and perfume.

"What are you wearing?"

"My yellow dress from the boteek."

"I mean perfume, dummy."

"I can't pronounce it," Ella called from the kitchen. *"Jardins de Bagatelle."*

"That's it. The bagatelle part is OK. I used to play bagatelle. But I just pointed and said, 'That one.' I was trying testers at Krim's. Do you like it?"

"Yes. I stole some last night."

"What?"

"Never mind."

Ann raised a leg languidly and looked up along it as if sighting. She spread out her toes fanwise to make sights, closed them together, spread them. "Exercises, exercises, *always* *do* your *exercises*," she chanted, raising the other leg. "Zhardang, zhardang it all to bagatelle."

"What?"

"Nothing, Ma!"

Ella clipped back into the living room with a vase of red cannas. "I see London, I see France," she observed.

"I'm exercising. When Stephen Sandman comes I'll lie here and do breathing exercises, ha-ah-ha-ah-ha-ah-ha-ah. Who is he?"

"Sandies. He's in Accounting. I asked him to come in for a drink before we go out."

"Go out where?"

"The new Vietnamese place. They only have a beer and wine license."

"Is he nice? Stephen Sandpiper?"

"I don't know him well," Ella said primly. "That is, of course we've known each other at the office slightly for years. He and his wife were divorced a couple of years ago now."

"Ha-ah-ha-ah-ha-ah," Ann said.

Ella stood back from the arrangement of cannas. "Do they look all right?"

"Terrific. What do you want to do about me? Shall I lie here showing my underpants and doing puppy breathing?"

"We'll sit out on the patio, I thought."

"Then the cannas are just for the walk-through."

"And you're very welcome to join us, dear."

"We could impress this guy," Ann said, sitting up and assuming half-lotus position. "I could put on an apron and be the maid. Do we have an apron? One of those little white cap things. I could serve the canapés. Canapé, Mr. Sandpuppy? Canopee, Mr. Sandpoopoo?"

"Oh, hush," her mother said. "You're silly. I hope it'll be warm enough on the patio." She clipped back to the kitchen.

"If you really want to impress him," Ann called, "you'd better hide me."

Ella appeared instantly in the doorway, her mouth drawn in, her small blue eyes burning like the lights on airfields. "I will not listen to you talk that way, Ann!"

"I meant, I'm such a slob, my panties show, I haven't washed my hair, and look at the bottoms of my feet, God."

Ella continued to glare for a moment, then turned and went back into the kitchen. Ann hauled herself out of half-lotus and onto her feet. She came to the kitchen doorway.

"I just thought maybe you'd rather be alone. You know."

"I would like him to meet my daughter," Ella said, fiercely mashing cream cheese.

"I'll get dressed. You smell terrific. He'll die, you know." Ann snuffled around the base of her mother's neck, the creamy, slightly freckled skin in which two soft, round creases appeared when she turned her head, weakly crying, "Don't, don't, it tickles!"

"Vamp," Ann whispered hotly behind her mother's ear.

"Stop!"

Ann went off to the bathroom and showered. Enjoying the sound and the steam and the sluicing of the hot water, she took a long time about it. As she came naked out into the hallway she heard a man's voice and leaped back into the bathroom, pulling the door shut, then reopening it slightly to listen. They had got about as far as the cannas. She slipped out of the bathroom and down the hall to her room. She pulled on bikinis and the T-shirt dress that slithered pleasantly on her skin and embraced her rounded belly in forgiving shapelessness. She blowdried her hair on hot while she teased it with her fingers, put on lipstick and wiped it off, checked in the long mirror, and went sedate and barefoot down the hall, past the cannas, out onto the little flagged terrace.

Stephen Sandies, wearing a cool grey canvas sports coat and white shirt without tie, stood up and gave her a firm handshake. His smile was white but not too. Dark hair greying nicely. Trim, tan, fit, around fifty, stern mouth but not pursy, everything under control. Cool, but not sweating to keep cool. Would do. Good going, Ma, pour on the Zhardang de Big Hotel! Ann winked at her mother, who recrossed her ankles and said, "I forgot the lemonade, dear, if that's what you want? It's in the icebox." Ella was the last person in the Western Industrial Hegemony who said icebox, or canapé, or crossed her legs at the ankles. When Ann returned with a glass of lemonade, Stephen was talking. She sat down in a white webbed chair. Quietly, like a good girl. She sipped. They were on their second margaritas. Stephen's voice was soft, with a kind of burring or slight huskiness in it, very sexy, a kind voice. Drink your lemonade now like a good girl and slope off. Slope off where? The belly telly in the bedroom? Shit. Forget it. Hang on, it's been a nice day. Keep playing tag in Bagatelle Gardens. Can't catch me. What was he saying about his son?

"Well," he said, and fetched a sigh. Fetched it from deep inside, a long haul. He looked up at Ella with the wry, dry grin appropriate to the question, "Do you really want to hear all this?"

She's supposed to say no?

"Yes," Ella said.

"Well, it's a long, dull story, really. Legal battles are dull. Not like Hollywood courtroom scenes. To put it as briefly as possible, when Marie and I separated I was so angry and so . . . bewildered, really, that I agreed to several arrangements too hastily. To put it briefly, I've been forced to the conclusion that she's not fit to bring up my son. So we're into the classic custody battle. I'd rather, frankly, that she didn't even have visiting rights, but I'll compromise if I have to. Judges favor the mother, of course. But I intend to win. And I will. My lawyers are very good. If only the process were faster. It's very painful to me to wait through the delays and procedures. Every day he's with her will have to be undone. It's as if it were a disease for which there is a cure, and I have the cure. But they won't let me have him to begin the cure." Wow. So much conviction, and so quiet. So certain. Ann studied his face briefly sidelong. Handsome, stern, kind, sad, like God. Was he possibly very very very conceited? Was he possibly right?

"Is it—Is she drinking?" Ella hazarded, sounding weak, and setting down her glass.

"Not to the point of alcoholism," Stephen replied in his gently measured way. He looked down into his margarita-slush. "You know, I don't like to say these things. We were married for eleven years. There were good times."

"Oh, yes," Ella murmured pathetically, squirming with the pain his understatement concealed. But why didn't *he* squirm?

"But," he said. "Well. Far be it from me! God knows. No job, but a credit card—Where my child-support payments go I don't know. Three schools for Todd in two years. Disorder, bohemianism—but if that were all—it isn't that. It's the exposure of my child to immorality."

Ann was terrified. She had not expected this. Debt, dirt, disorder, OK, but immorality—her child would be exposed, exposed to immorality. Naked, soft, helpless, exposed. She would expose it by giving birth to it. By being its mother she would expose it to the dirt, the disorder, the immorality of a woman's life, her life. Its father would come from Riverside with a court order on clean, white paper. It would be taken from her, taken into custody. She would never see it. No visiting rights. No birth rights. It would be stillborn, it would die of immorality even before she could expose it.

Ella's mouth was drawn in, her eyes cast down. Stephen had

just said a word to her that explained all. And Ann had not been listening. Had the word been "woman"?

"You see why I can't leave the boy there," Stephen said, and though not squirming he was in pain, no doubt of it, his hand tight on the arm of the chair.

Ella shook her head in agreement.

"And this—woman's friends. All—the same kind. Flaunting it."

Ann saw the monstrous regiment.

Stephen's head moved in tiny, rigid spasms as he spoke. "And the boy alone, in that. With them. Eight years old. A good kid. Straight as an arrow. I can't. I can't stand. To think of him. With them. Learning. That."

Each staccato burst hit Ann like machine-gun fire. She set down her lemonade glass on the flagstone, got carefully to her feet, and slipped away from Margaritaville with a vague smile, bleeding, bleeding evil monthly blood, nine months' worth bleeding from the holes he had shot in her. Behind her, her mother's voice said something consolatory to the man and then was raised, thin and weak, to cry, "Ann?"

"Back in a minute, Mama."

Passing the cannas flaming in twilight, she heard Ella say, "Ann is taking a year off from college. She's five months pregnant." She spoke in a strange tone, warning, boastful. Flaunting.

Ann went on to the bathroom. She had left her old underpants and shorts and T-shirt all over the bathroom when she showered, and he would have come to pee before they left and seen them and then her mother would have too and died. She picked things up. The bullet holes had been closed by her mother's voice. The blood had sublimated and etherealised into tears. She snivelled as she dropped dirty clothes and wet towels into the dirty-clothes hamper, she cried gratefully, she washed her face and opened the bottle of Jardins de Bagatelle, the perfume of the mother tiger, and put it on her hands and on her face where she could smell it.

LIVING IN YINLAND

Duffy slung on her knapsack and went out, saying over her shoulder, "Back around seven."

Her motorcycle revving and roaring off left silence behind. The Sunday paper was all over the living room. Nobody had got up till after noon.

"God, you know," Ella said, dropping the comics, "we get our periods exactly the same time now, within a day?"

"Hey, yeah? I've heard of that. That's kind of neat."

"Yeah, only I was beginning to stop having periods most of the time. Oh well. Tit for tat, as they say." Ella snorted. "I want some more coffee." She got up and shuffled off to the kitchen. "You want some?" she called.

"Not now."

Ella shuffled back in. She wore pink feather mules with low heels that flopped off if she lifted her foot.

"Those are really frivolous, El. I mean seriously frivolous."

"Duffy ordered them for me from some mail order catalogue." Ella sat down on the couch again, set her coffee cup on the table, and lifted one leg to look at the slipper. "She thought they'd suit me. Actually it's kind of like the things Stephen used to buy me sometimes. Mistakes."

"Like the stuff you make at school and then your parents have to use them."

"Like women buying men ties, it really is true. I love paisley and Stephen hated it, he thought paisley looked like bugs, those curvy sort of shapes, you know, and I didn't realise it and I always bought him these beautiful paisley ties."

"Isn't it weird how . . ."

"How what?"

"I don't know, how we don't get through to each other, you know, only we sort of do, only not where we thought we were. I mean, like you're *wearing* those. Well, and like both of us thinking the other one would like disapprove, and all that stuff you went through psyching yourself up to call me about selling Mother's house. Everything backwards. But it works. Sometimes."

"Yeah," Ella said. "Sometimes." She had put both pink-feathered feet up on the edge of the coffee table, and gazed at them, her small, bright, light-blue eyes stern, judgmental. Her half-sister Ann, a much larger woman fifteen years younger, sat on the floor amidst the comics and classifieds and coffee cups, wearing purple sweatpants and a red sweatshirt with an expressionless yellow circle-face on it labelled, "Have A Day."

"Mom used that chicken ashtray I made in fourth grade till she died," Ella said.

"Even after she quit smoking. El, did you like my dad?"

Ella gazed at her feet. "Yeah," she said. "I liked him. You know, I didn't ever remember a whole lot about my own father. I was only six when he got killed and he'd been overseas a year. I don't think I even cried except because Mom cried. So I wasn't comparing, or anything. I guess what I didn't like when Mom and Bill married was I missed her and me being together. Like this, you know, slopping around. Women slopping around. That's partly why I like it with Duffy. Only Duffy's more, well, it has to do with sex, not gender, I guess. With Duffy it's not so easy, you have to watch it. With Mom it was so easy. With you it's easy."

"Too easy, sort of?"

"I don't know. Maybe. I like it, though. Anyhow. I wasn't ever jealous of Bill or anything. He was a sweet guy. I guess in fact I had a crush on him for a while. Trying to compete with Mom. Practicing . . ."

Ella's smile, which was infrequent, curved her long, thin lips into a charming half-circle.

"I got a crush on everybody. My math teacher. The bus driver. The paper boy. God, I used to get up in the dark and wait at the window to see the paper boy."

"Always men?"

Ella nodded. "They hadn't invented women yet, then," she said.

Ann stretched out flat on the floor and raised first one purple leg, pointing her toes at the ceiling, then the other.

"What were you when you got married? Nineteen?" she asked.

"Nineteen. Young. Younger than, Christ, fresh eggs. But you know, I wasn't really dumb. I mean Stephen was a really good guy, I mean a prince. You probably only remember him after he was drinking."

"I remember your wedding."

"Oh Christ yes, when you were flower girl."

"And that little fart son of Aunt Marie's was ring bearer, and we got into a fight."

"Oh God yes, and Marie started crying and saying she never thought to have people in the *family* who were *minorities*, and Mom got mad and said why not call Bill a spick straight out then, and Marie did, she started yelling, 'A spick then! A spick then!' And she had hysterics, and Bill's brother the vet got her squiffed in the vestry. No wonder things went wrong with a start like that. But I did want to say about Steve, he was a really, really bright, lovely guy. See, I can't say that to Duffy. It would just hurt her for no reason. She isn't very secure. But sometimes I need to say it, to be fair to him, and to myself. Because it was so unfair what being alcoholic did to him. And you know, I had to finally just get out and run. And for me that was OK, it's worked out fine. But I think of how he started out and how he ended up, and it, I don't know, it isn't fair."

"You ever hear from him any more?"

Ella shook her head. "I've been thinking the last year or so he's probably dead," she said in the same quiet voice. "He was down so far. But I won't ever know."

"Was he the only guy you went with seriously?"

Ella nodded one nod.

After a while, looking at her pink-feathered feet, she said,

"Sex with a drunk is not the biggest turn-on. I don't guess anybody but Duffy could of got through to me, maybe." She blushed, a delicate but vivid pink appearing suddenly in her rather sallow cheeks and fading slowly. "Duffy's a very kind person," she said.

"I like her," Ann said.

Ella sighed. She slid her feet out of the feathered mules, letting them drop to the floor, and curled herself up on the couch. "What is this, true confession time?" she said. "I was wanting to ask you how come you didn't want to stay with the baby's father, was he a jerk or something."

"Oh God."

"I'm sorry."

"No. It's just embarrassing to say. Todd's seventeen. Eighteen by now, I guess. One of my Computer Programming students." Ann sat up and bowed her head down to her knees, stretching tension out of her back and hiding her face, then sat up straight; she was smiling.

"Does he know?"

"Nope."

"Did you think about an abortion at all?"

"Oh, yeah. But see. It was me that was careless. So I wondered, why was I careless? And I wanted to quit teaching anyhow. And get out of Riverside. I want to stay around the Bay here and get work. Temping to start with, till I find what I want. I can always find a job, that's no problem for me. I want to get into programming eventually, and maybe consulting. I can have the baby and then go back part time. And I want to live alone with the baby and kind of take my time. Because I kept sort of rushing into everything, you know? But what I think is I'm a maternal type, actually, more than a wife type or a lover type."

"Could take some finding out," Ella said.

"Well, that's why I want to sort of slow down. But I'll tell you my long-range plans. I'll find this executive, fifty, fifty up, maybe sixty up, and marry him. Mommy marries Daddy, see?" She bowed her head to her knees again and came up smiling.

"Dumb, dumb, dumb," Ella said. "Dumb shit sister. You can leave the baby here on your honeymoon."

"With Auntie Ella."

"And Uncle Duffy. Christ. I haven't seen Duffy with a baby."

"Is Duffy her real name?"

"She'd kill me if she knew I told you. Marie."

"Cross my heart."

They unfolded and refolded various sections of the paper, leafed slowly. Ann looked at pictures of resorts in the Northern Coast Range, read advertisements from travel agencies, fly to Hawaii, cruise Alaska.

"What ever happened to that little fart son of Aunt Marie's, anyhow?"

"Wayne. He got some degree in Business Administration at UCLA."

"It figures."

"What are you? Pisces?"

"I think so."

"It says this is a good day for you to make long-range plans, and look out for an important Scorpio. That's your sugar daddy, I guess."

"No, what's November, is that Scorpio?"

"Yeah. Till the twenty-fourth, it says."

"OK, that's this long-range plan in here. I'll look out for it. . . ."

After a pause Ella, reading, said, "Seventeen."

"*All* right," Ann said, reading.

MIRRORING

The lower edge of the lawn above the riverbank was planted in red cannas. Beyond that intense color the river was gunbarrel blue. Both the red line and the blue reflected in Stephen's mirror-finish sun glasses, moving up and down across the surface and seeming to change the expression of his face incomprehensibly. Todd looked away from this display with an irritable turn of the head. Stephen asked at once, "What's wrong?"

"I wish you didn't wear mirror shades."

"See yourself reflected in them?" Smiling, Stephen slowly took the glasses off. "Is that so bad?"

"What I see is all these colors running across your face like some robot in the movies. Mirror shades are like aggressive, you know? Black dudes coming on cool. Hank Williams Junior."

"If you're behind them, they're defensive. Soft-bodied animal hiding. Protective mimicry. I bought them for this trip." Stephen's face without the glasses did look soft, not doughy or rubbery but soft-finished like stone or wood long used, worn down to fineness. All the lines that etched his face were fine, and the cut of lip and nostril and eyelid was delicate but blurred by that softening, that abrasion of years. Todd looked down at his own big, smooth hands and knees and thighs with a sense of self-consciousness that sharpened to discomfort. He looked back at Stephen's hands holding the sun glasses.

"No, you're right," Stephen said, "they're aggressive." He was holding them so that the curved, insectile planes reflected his own face and behind it the white facade of the hotel against the dark mountain. "I see you—you don't see me. . . . But I want to look at you all the time. And with these on, I can do just that. And you don't have to see as much of me."

"I like seeing you," Todd said, but Stephen was fitting the glasses back across his face.

"Now I can be contemplating the river, for all *they* know, while all the time inside here I'm actually staring, staring, staring at you, trying to get my fill. . . . I don't believe you. I can't believe you. That you came. That you wanted to come. That you wanted to give me this incredible gift. I have to wear these when I look at you. You are nineteen years old. I could go blind. You don't have to say anything. Letting me say these things is your gift to me. Part of your gift to me." When he wore the mirroring glasses his voice was smoother, softer, deflecting answers.

Todd said doggedly, "The giving goes the other way too. Mostly, in fact."

"No, no, no," Stephen murmured. "Nothing. Nothing."

"All this?" Todd looked around at the red cannas, the white hotel, the dark ridges, the river.

"All this," Stephen repeated. "Plus Miz Gertrude and Miz Alice B. My God, those women follow us like reflections in a funnyhouse. Don't look!"

Todd was already looking over his shoulder to see the two women coming up the path between the lawns from the river. The old one was in the lead and the young one a good ways behind her, carrying fishing poles. Seeing him turn, the old one held up a couple of good-sized trout and called out something ending with "breakfast!"

Todd nodded and made a V for Victory sign.

"They catch fish," Stephen murmured. "They beach whales. They play five-card stud. They fell giant sequoias. They deploy missiles. They gut bears. Only please God let them stay busy and leave us alone! A fish-waving bull dyke is more than I can cope with just now. Tell me that they're going away."

"They're going away."

"Good. Good." The curved black surfaces turned again, canna-red flashing across them. "They'll have vacated the rowboat we were hoping for, presumably. Shall we go on the river?"

"Sure." Todd stood up.

"Do you want to, Tadziu?"

Todd nodded.

"You do whatever I ask or suggest. You should do what *you* like. Your pleasure is my pleasure."

"Let's go."

"Let's go," Stephen repeated, smiling, standing up.

On the lazy water of the lake above the dam, Todd shipped the oars and slid down to lie with his back against the seat.

Behind him Stephen's husky voice sang in a whisper, "*Dans les jardins de mon père . . .*" and then, after a silence, spoke softly aloud:

> "*Ame, te souvient-il, au fond du paradis,*
> *De la gare d'Auteuil, et des trains de jadis?*"

"No assignments on spring break," Todd said.

"No one could translate it in any case."

Todd felt Stephen's finger like a feather caress the outer rim of his left ear, once.

It was completely silent on the water. On his lips Todd tasted the salt of his sweat from rowing. Behind him Stephen sitting in the prow made no sound, said nothing.

"One of them left a fly box under the seat here," Todd said, looking down at it.

"Under no circumstances take it to them. I'll turn it in at the hotel desk. Or drop it overboard. It's the excuse they've been waiting for. It's a plant. Oh how kind of you we've just been dying to talk to you and your father and I'm Alice B and this is Gertie and isn't this place just bully for all us boys? It's called the dyke bursting."

Todd laughed. Again the feather touch went round his ear, and he laughed again, repressing a shudder of pleasure.

All he could see as he half lay in the boat was colorless sky and one long sunlit ridge.

"You know," he said, "I think actually you've got them wrong. The girl was talking last night to that girl Marie that cooks, you know? On the terrace, when I went out to smoke a joint, last night late, you know. And she was telling her she came here with her mother, because her brother died, and her mother had been nursing him, or something, like he was sick for a long time or like brain damaged or something. So when he died she wanted to bring her mother up here for a rest and like a change. So actually they'd be mother and daughter. I looked in the registration book when I came in and it said Ella Sanderson and Ann Sanderson."

The silence behind him continued. He tipped his head back and back till he could see Stephen's face upside down, the black sun glasses mirroring the sky.

"Does it matter?" Stephen's voice said, terribly melancholy.

"No."

Todd lifted his head and looked across the colorless water at the colorless sky beyond where the ridges narrowed in the dam.

"It doesn't matter at all," he said.

"I could sink the boat now," the sorrowful, tender voice behind him said. "Like a stone."

"OK."

"You understand . . . ?"

"Sure. This is the center. Like which is water and which is sky. So sinking's flying. It doesn't matter. At the center. Go on."

After a long time Todd sat back up on the seat, reset the oars, and began rowing in long, quiet strokes away from the lip of the dam. He did not look around.

EARTHWORKS

Ann's father had recently made a pond from a spring below the ranch house, and after lunch they walked down to see it. Horses grazed on the high, bare, golden hill on the far side of the water. From the rainy-season highwater line the banks were bare and muddy down to the summer level, making a reddish rim. A rowboat, looking oversized, was pulled up beside the tiny dock. They sat on the dock, in bathing suits, dangling their feet in the tepid water. They were too full of food and wine to want to swim yet. Although the baby did not yet crawl and was sound asleep anyhow, the knowledge that he was sleeping with water a foot or two away on either side of him was a dim unease in Ann's mind, making her look round at him quite frequently and keep one hand touching the flannel blanket he lay on. To hide her overprotectiveness or to excuse it from herself, each time she looked round at the baby she readjusted the cotton shirt which she had taken off and tented up over him to protect his head from the sun.

"Now," said her father, "I want to know about your life. The place you live. The woman you live with. Start there."

"Ground floor of an old house in San Pablo. Two bedrooms, and a walk-in closet for Toddie's room. Old Japanese couple have the upstairs. The neighborhood's a little rough but there's a lot of nice people, and our block is OK. OK? Then Marie. She's gay, but we're not living together. It's actually Toddie she was interested in."

"Jesus!"

"I mean, she wanted to help parent a baby." Ann broke into a laugh that was both genuine and nervous. "She does computer programming and counselling, so she works at home a lot. It works out really well for care-sharing. The way it works out with her and me, we each have a wife."

"Great," Stephen said.

"I mean, you know, a person you can count on to sort of take over if you can't. And do the shitwork, and you know."

"Not my experience of wives," her father said. "So you've given up on men, then."

"No. Like I said, Marie and I aren't together. She has lesbian friends, a lot of my friends are straight, but just now, I don't know, I'm just not into that a whole lot. I will again, you know. It's not like I'm bitter or anything. I wanted to have the baby. I just want to be with him mainly at this point. The job's weird hours, but that means when I'm out Marie's there, and mostly when he's awake, I'm there. So it's real good now. And later it'll change. . . ."

As she spoke she felt in her father, sitting a foot or two from her, a physical resistance, a great impatience; she felt it physically as a high, hard, slanting blade, like the blade of a bulldozer. The owner of the land had the right to clear it, to clear out this under-brush of odd jobs, half-couplings, rented closets, hiding places, makeshifts. The blade advanced.

"Since Penny and I divorced I've done a lot of stock-taking. Sitting right here. Or riding Dolly over there around the ranch." Her father was looking across the pond at the high hill as he spoke, watching the grazing mare and colt and the white gelding. "Thinking about both my marriages. Especially about the first one, strangely enough. I began to see that I didn't ever work through the whole thing before I married Penny. I never really handled the pain your mother caused me. I denied it. Macho, tough guy—real men don't feel pain. You can keep up that crap for years. But it finally catches up with you. And then you realise all you've done is save your shit to drown in. So I've been doing the work I should have done ten, twelve years ago. And some of it's almost too late. I have to face the fact that I wasted a lot of those years, wasted a marriage. Started it and ended it in all the unfinished business from the first marriage. Well, OK. Win one, lose one. What I'm doing now is establishing priorities. What's important. What comes first. And doing that, I've been able to see what my mistake, my one real mistake, was. You know what it was?"

He looked at her so keenly with his clear, light-blue eyes that she flinched. He waited, smiling slightly, alert.

"Divorcing Mama, I guess," she said, looking down and swal-lowing the words because she knew they were wrong. He did not speak, and she looked back at him. He was still smiling, and she thought what a handsome man he was, looking like a Roman general now with his short-cropped hair and silver-blue eyes, long lips and eagle nose, but wearing a Plains Indian beaded talisman on a rawhide cord about his neck. He was very deeply tanned. On his ranch in summer he wore nothing but shorts and thong san-dals, or went naked.

"That was no mistake," he said. "That was one of the right things I did. And buying this place. I had to move *on*. And Ella isn't willing, isn't able to go on, to act, move, develop. Her strength is in staying put. God, what strength! But it's all in that. So the shit piles up around her, and she never clears it away. Hell, she builds walls of it! Fecal fortifications. Defending her from, God forbid, change. From, God forbid, freedom . . . I had to break out of her fortress. I was suffocating. Buried alive. I tried to take her with me. She wouldn't come. Wouldn't move. Ella never had any use for freedom, her own or anybody else's. And I was so desperate for it by then that I'd take it on any terms. So that's where I made my mistake."

She felt remiss at still not understanding what his mistake had been, but he said nothing, and she was obliged to admit it: "I guess I don't know what mistake," she said, feeling as she said it that it must have something to do with her, and oppressed by the feeling. She glanced over her shoulder at the sleeping baby.

"Leaving you," her father said quietly. "Not putting up a fight for custody."

She knew that this was very important to him and ought to be so to her, but all she felt was that she was being crowded, pushed along by the slanting, uprooting blade, and she looked back again at the baby and moved the shirttail unnecessarily to shade his legs.

"A little late to think about that, she thinks," her father's voice said gently.

"Oh, I don't know. Anyhow we got to see each other every summer," she said, blushing red.

The blade moved forward, levelling and making clear. "I needed freedom in order to go on living, and I saw you as part of the jail. Part of Ella. I *literally* didn't separate you from her—you see? She didn't allow that possibility even as an idea. You were her, you were her motherhood, and she was the Great Mother. She had you built right into the walls. And I bought that. Maybe if you'd been a boy I'd have seen what was going on sooner. I'd have felt my part in you, my claim—my right to get you out of the shit-fort, the earthworks. *My* right to assert *your* right to freedom. You see? But I didn't see it. I didn't look. I just got loose and left you as hostage. It's taken me twelve years to be able to admit that. I want you to know that I do admit it now."

Ann picked a foxtail from the corner of the baby's blanket by her hip. "Yeah, well," she said. "I guess it worked out OK, anyhow, you know, Mom and me, and anyhow Penny didn't want some teen-age stepdaughter around all the time."

"If I'd fought for you and won custody—and if I'd fought I'd have won—what Penny wanted or didn't want would have been a matter of supreme indifference. I probably wouldn't have married her. One mistake leads to the next one. You'd have lived here. All your summers here. Gone to a good school. And a four-year college, maybe an Eastern school, Smith or Vassar. And you wouldn't be living with a lesbian in San Pablo, working nights for a phone company. I'm not blaming you, I'm blaming myself. I can't believe how true to form Ella is, how unchangingly unchanging—how she dug you in, walled you into the same dirt, the same futureless trap. What kind of future does your life spell for your kid, Ann?"

But I was really lucky to get the job, Ann thought, but what's neat is that for a while things aren't changing all the time, but you haven't even seen Mom for ten years so how do you know? All these thoughts were mere shadows and underbrush, among which her mind hopped like a rabbit.

"Well," she said, "things are really OK the way they worked out," and, unable to control her increasing anxiety about Toddie, she turned away from her father and knelt above the sleeping baby, pretending that he had waked up. "All right then! Up you come! Hey baby bunny boy. Hey you sleepy bunny." The baby's head wobbled, his eyes looked in different directions, and as soon as she settled him on her lap he fell fast asleep again. His small, warm, neat weight gave her substance. She stirred the lake with her toes and said, "You shouldn't worry about it, Daddy. I'm really happy. I just wish you were, if you aren't."

"You're happy," he said, with one glance of his light eyes, the almost scornfully accurate touch she remembered, that reversed the poles.

"Yes, I am," she said. "But there's one thing I wanted to tell you about."

While she summoned up words, Stephen said, with satisfaction in his acuteness, "I thought so. The father's back in the picture."

"No," Ann said vaguely, not heeding. "Well, see, they think at the clinic that Toddie had some brain damage, probably at birth. That's why he's slow developing in some ways. We noticed it pretty soon. They can't tell how much yet, and they think it isn't real severe. But they know there's some impairment." She drew her fingertip very lightly around the tiny pink curve of the baby's ear. "So. That's taken some, you know, thinking. Getting used to. It's not as big a deal as I thought. But it is, in some ways."

"What are you doing about it?"

"There isn't anything to do. Now. Sort of wait and see. And watch. He's only five months. They noticed a—"

"What are you doing about correcting it?"

"There isn't anything like that to do."

"You're just going to take this?"

She was silent.

"Ann, this is my grandson."

She nodded.

"Don't cut me out. You may be angry at the father, but don't take it out on men, don't join the castraters, for God's sake! Let me help. Let me get some competent doctors, let's get some light on this. Don't dig down into a hole with all these fears and old wives' tales, and smother the kid with them. I don't accept this. Not on the word of some midwife at this women's clinic that botched the kid's birth! My God, Ann! You can't take this out on *him!* There are things that can be done!"

"I've taken him to Permanente," Ann said.

"Shit! Permanente! You need first-class doctors, specialists, neurologists—Bill can give us some recommendations. I'll get onto it when we go back to the house. I'll call him. My God. This is what I meant! This is it. This is what I left you in—the mud—My God! how could you sit here all day with him and me and *not tell me?*"

"It isn't your fault, Daddy."

"Yes," he said, "it is. Exactly. If I—"

She interrupted. "It's the way he is. And there's a best way for him to be, like anybody. And that's what we can do, is find that. So please don't talk shit about 'correcting.' Look, I'd like to have a swim now, I think. Will you hold him?"

She saw that he was startled, even frightened, but he said nothing. She carefully transferred the rosy, sweaty, silky baby onto his thin thighs covered with sparse sun-bleached hairs. She saw his large, fine hand cup the small head. She got up then and went three steps to the end of the little dock and stood on the weather-gnawed grey planks. The water was shallow, and she did not dive but splashed down in, her feet tangling for a moment in slimy weeds. She swam. Ten or fifteen yards out she turned, floated awhile, trod water to look back at the dock. Stephen sat motionless in the flood of sunlight, his head bowed over the baby, whom she could not even see in the shadow of her father's body.

THE PHOTOGRAPH

As she was scrubbing out the kitchen sink, where she had let bleaching powder stand to whiten the old rust stains, Ella saw that the girl from the complex was talking with Stephen. She rinsed out the sink, got her dark glasses from the kitchen oddments drawer, polished them a bit with the dishtowel, put them on, and went out into the back yard.

Stephen was weeding the vegetable plot by the fence, and the girl was standing on the other side of the fence, just her head and shoulders showing. She had her baby in one of those kangaroo things that mashed it up against its mother's front. It was asleep, nothing visible but the tiny sleek head like a kitten's back. Stephen was working, his head bent down as usual, and didn't seem to be paying attention to the girl, but just as she came out, before the screen door banged, Ella heard him say, "Green beans."

The girl looked up and said, "Oh, hi, Mrs. Hoby!" in a bright voice. Stephen kept his head bent down at his weeding.

Ella came over to the laundry roundabout and felt the clothes she had hung out earlier in the afternoon. Stephen's T-shirts and her yellow wash dress were dry already, but Stephen's jeans were still damp, as she had expected; feeling them was nothing but an excuse for coming out.

"You sure have a nice garden," the girl said.

The complex of eight apartments they had built next door ten years ago had nothing but cement and garages behind it where the Pannis's garden with the big jacaranda had been. There was no place for a child to play there. But before the baby was old enough the girl would have moved on, the welfare-and-food-stamp people never stayed, the men with no jobs and the girls with no husbands, playing their big radio-tape machines loud and smoking dope at night in those hot little apartments.

"Stephen and I know each other from the store," the girl said. "He carried my groceries home for me last week. That was a nice thing to do. I had the baby, and my arms were just about falling off."

Stephen laughed his "huh-huh," not looking up.

"Have you lived here for a long time?" the girl asked. Ella was rehanging the jeans, for something to do. She answered after she had got the seams matched. "My brother has lived here all his life. This is his house."

"It is? That's neat," the girl said. "All his *life*? That's amazing! How old are you, Stephen?"

Ella thought he would not answer, and it might serve the girl right, but after a considerable pause he said, "Four. Forty-four."

"Forty-four years right here? That's wonderful. It's a nice house, too."

"It was," Ella said. "It was all single-family houses when we were children here." She spoke dryly, but she had to admit that the girl did not mean to patronise, and was pleasant, the way she talked right to Stephen instead of across him the way most people did, or else they shouted at him as if he were deaf, which he was only slightly, in the right ear.

Stephen stood up, dusted off his knees carefully, and went across the grass and into the house, hooking the screen door shut behind him with his foot.

Ella had sat down on the small cement base of the laundry roundabout to pull at a dandelion clump in the grass. It had been there for years, always coming back. You had to get every single piece of root of a dandelion, and the roots went under the cement.

"Did I hurt his feelings?" the girl asked, shifting the baby in its carrier.

"No," Ella said. "He's probably getting a photograph to show you. Of the house."

"I really like him," the girl said. Her voice was low and a little husky, with a break in it, like some children's voices. What they used to call a whiskey voice, only childlike. The poor thing was not much more than a child. Babies having babies, they had said on the television.

"Have you always lived here too, Mrs. Hoby?"

Ella worked at the dandelion root, loosening it, then took off her sun glasses and looked round at the girl. "My husband and I ran a resort hotel," she said. "Up in the redwood country, on a river. A very old place, built in the eighteen eighties, quite well known. We owned it for twenty-seven years. When my husband passed away I ran it for two more years. Then when my mother passed away and left the house to Stephen, I decided to retire and come live here with him. He has never lived with strangers. He's fifty-four, not forty-four. Numbers confuse him sometimes."

The girl listened intently. "Did you have to sell the resort? Do you still own it?"

"I sold it," Ella said.

"What was it like?"

"A big country hotel, up north. Twenty-six rooms. High ceilings. A terraced dining room over the river. We had to modernise the kitchens and the plumbing entirely when we bought it. There used to be places like that. Elegant. Before the motels. People came for a week, or a month. Some people, families and single people, came every summer or fall for years. They made their reservation for the next year before they left. We offered fishing, good trout fishing, and horseback riding, and mountain walks. It was called The Old River Inn. It's mentioned in several books. The present owners call it a 'bed and breakfast.'" Ella dug her fingers in under the dandelion root, sinewy there in its dirt darkness, and pried. It broke. She should have got the weeder or the garden fork.

"What an amazing kind of thing to do," the girl said, "running a place like that." Ella could have told her that they had never had a vacation themselves for a quarter of a century and that the hotel had worn her out and finally killed Bill and eaten up their lives for nothing, mortgaged and remortgaged and the payments from the bed and breakfast people not even enough to live on here, but because there was a break or a catch in the girl's voice that sounded as if she saw the forest ridges and the Inn on its lawns above the river as Ella saw it, as the old, noble, beautiful, remote thing, she said only, "It was hard work," but smiled a little as she said it.

Stephen came out of the house and straight across the grass, glancing up once at the girl and then down again at the picture he held. It was the framed photograph of Mama and Papa on the porch of the house, the year they bought it, and Ella in her pinafore dress sitting on the top front step, and Baby Stephen sitting in the pram. The girl took it and looked at it for quite a time.

"That's Mama. That's Papa. That's Ella. That's me, the baby," he said, and laughed quietly, "huh-huh!"

The girl laughed too and sniffled and wiped her nose and her eyes quite openly. "Look how little all the trees are!" she said.

"You've been doing a lot of gardening since they took that picture, I guess." She handed it carefully back across the fence to Stephen. "Thank you for showing it to me," she said, and her little whiskey voice was so sad that Ella turned her head away and scraped her nails in the dirt trying to seize the broken root, in vain, till the girl had gone, because there was nothing to say to her but what she knew already.

THE STORY

Ann sat erect in the white-painted iron chair on the little flagged terrace behind the house. She wore white, and was barefoot. The old abelia bushes behind her, above the terrace, were in full flower. Her child sat among scattered plastic toys on the edge of the terrace where it met the lawn, near her. Ella looked at them from the kitchen window, through the yellow metal blinds that were slanted to send the hot afternoon light upward to the ceiling, making the low room glow like the wax of a lighted beeswax candle. Todd moved the toys about, but she could not see a pattern in the way he moved or placed them; they did not seem to relate to each other. He did not talk when he picked up one or another. There was no story being told. He dropped an animal figure and picked up a broken-off dandelion flower, dropped it. Only from time to time he made a humming or droning noise, loud enough that Ella could hear it pretty clearly, a rhythmic, nasal sound, "Anh-hanh, anh-hanh, hanh . . ." When he was making this music of his he swayed or rocked a little and his face, half hidden by thick glasses, brightened and relaxed. He was a pretty child.

His mother, Ann, was very beautiful there in the sunlight, her pale skin shining with sweat, her dark hair loose and bright against the shadow and the small, pale, creamy flowers of the abelia. Had she given promise of such beauty? Ella had thought her rather plain as a child, but then she had held herself back from the child, not looking for her beauty, knowing that if she found it

34

all it meant was losing it, since Stephen and Marie came West so seldom, and after the divorce Marie never wanted to send the child alone. Three or four years would pass when she never saw Ann. And a grandchild's life goes by so fast, faster than a child's.

Stephen had been a pretty child, now! People had stopped her to admire him in his little blue and white suit in the pram, or when he was walking and held her hand and walked with her down to the old Cash and Carry Market. His blue eyes were so bright and clear, and his fair hair curled all over his head. And that innocent look some little boys have, that trusting look, he had kept that so long, right into his teens, really. And how Stephen had told stories when he was this child's age! From morning till night there had been some tale going, till it drove her crazy sometimes, Stephen babbling softly away at table, anywhere, telling his unending saga about the Wood Dog and what was it?—the Puncha. The Puncha, and other characters he had made up out of his head. They didn't have the TV then, or the bright plastic toys, soldiers and tanks and monsters. While they lived up on the ranch, Stephen had had no playmates at all, unless Shirley brought her girls over for the day. So he told his endless adventures, which Ella could never understand, playing with a toy car or two and bits of mill ends for blocks, or an old spool, wooden the way spools were, and wooden clothespins, and the little husky monotone voice: "So they went up there rrrrrm, rrrrrm, rrrrrm, and they were waiting there, so they went along there, rrrrrm, rrrrrm, so then the road stopped and they fell off, they fell down, down, down, help help where's Puncha?" And so on and on like that, even in his bed at night.

"Stephen?"

"Yes Mama!"

"Hush now and go to sleep!"

"I *am* asleep, Mama!" Virtuous indignation. She hid her laugh. She tiptoed to the door, and in a minute the little voice would begin to whisper again: "So then they said Let's go to the, to the lake. So there was this boat on the lake and so then Wood Dog started sinking, crash, splash, help help where's Puncha? Here I am Wood Dog. . . ." Then at last a small yawn. Then silence.

Where did all that go? What happened to it? The funny little boy making everything in the world into his story, he never would have understood any story about a telephone company executive recently married for the third time whose only child by his first marriage was sitting now in the white chair watching her only child by no marriage rock back and forth restlessly and endlessly, droning his music of one nasal syllable.

"Ann," Ella said, lifting the slatted blind, "diet cola or lemonade?"

"Lemonade, Grandmother."

What became of it? she asked again, getting the ice out of the refrigerator, getting the glasses down from the cupboard. Why didn't the story make sense? Such hope she had had for Stephen, so sure he would do something noble. Not a word people used, and of course it was silly to expect a happy ending. Would it have been better to be like poor young Ann, who had no hope or pride beyond the most austere realism—"He won't be fully self-sufficient, but his dependence level can be reduced a good deal. . . ." Was it better, more honest, to tell only very short stories, like that? Were all the others mere lies, romances?

She put the two tall tumblers and the plastic cup on a tray, filled them with ice and lemonade, then clicked her tongue at herself in disgust, took the ice out of Todd's cup, and refilled it with plain lemonade. She put four animal crackers in a row on the tray and carried it out, batting the screen door shut behind her with her foot. Ann stood up and took the tray from her and set it down on the wobbly iron table, its curlicues clogged solid with years of repainting with white enamel, but still rusting through in spots.

"Can someone have the cookies?" Ella inquired softly.

"Oh, yes," Ann said. "Oh, very much yes. Todd. Look what's here. Look what Grandmother brought you!"

The thick little glasses peered round. The child got up and came to the table.

"Grandmother will give you a cookie, Todd," the young mother said, clear and serious.

The child stood still.

Ella picked up an animal cracker. "Here you are, sweetie," she said. "It's a tiger, I do believe. Here comes the tiger, walking to you." She walked the cracker across the tray, hopped it over the edge of the tray, and walked it onto the table's edge. She was not sure the four-year-old was watching.

"Take it, Todd," the mother said.

Slowly the child raised his open hand towards the table.

"Hop!" Ella said, hopping the tiger into the hand.

Todd looked at the tiger and then at his mother.

"Eat it, Todd. It's very good."

The child stood still, the cracker lying on his palm. He looked at it again. "Hop," he said.

"That's right! It went Hop! right to Toddie!" Ella said. Tears came into her eyes. She walked the next cracker across the tray. "This one is a pig. It can go Hop! too, Toddie. Do you want it to go Hop?"

"Hop!" the child said.

It was better than no story at all.

"Hop!" said the great-grandmother.

THE PROFESSOR'S HOUSES

For Tony

The professor had two houses, one inside the other. He lived with his wife and child in the outer house, which was comfortable, clean, disorderly, not quite big enough for all his books, her papers, their daughter's bright deciduous treasures. The roof leaked after heavy rains early in the fall before the wood swelled, but a bucket in the attic sufficed. No rain fell upon the inner house, where the professor lived without his wife and child; or so he said jokingly sometimes: "Here's where I live. My house." His daughter often added, without resentment, for the visitor's information, "It started out to be for me, but it's really his." And she might reach in to bring forth an inch-high table lamp with fluted shade, or a blue dish the size of her little fingernail, marked "Kitty" and half full of eternal milk; but she was sure to replace these, after they had been admired, pretty near exactly where they had been. The little house was very orderly, and just big enough for all it contained, though to some tastes the bric-à-brac in the parlor might seem excessive. The daughter's preference was for the store-bought gimmicks and appliances, the toasters and carpet sweepers of Lilliput, but she knew that most adult visitors would admire the perfection of the furnishings her father himself had so delicately and finely made and finished. He was inclined to be a little shy of showing off his own work, so she would point out the more ravishing elegances: the glass-fronted sideboard, the hardwood parquetry and the dadoes, the widow's walk. No visitor, child or adult, could withstand the fascination of the Venetian blinds, the infinitesimal slats that slanted and slid in perfect order on their cords of double-weight sewing thread. "Do you know how to make a Venetian blind?" the professor would inquire, setting up the visitor for his daughter, who would forestall or answer the hesitant negative with a joyful, "Put his eyes out!" Her father, who was entertained by involutions, and like all teachers willing to repeat a good thing, would then remark that after working for two weeks on those blinds, he had established that a Venetian blind can also make an American blind.

"I did that awful rug in the nursery," the professor's wife, Julia, might say, evidencing her participation in the inner house, her approbation, her incompetence. "It's not up to Ian's standard, but he accepted the intent." The crocheted rug was, in fact, coarse-looking and curly-edged; the needlepoint rugs in the other rooms, miniature Orientals and a gaudy floral in the master bedroom, lay flat and flawless.

The inner house stood on a low table in an open alcove, called "the bookshelf end," of the long living room of the outer house. Friends of the family checked the progress of its construction, furnishing, and fitting-out as they came to dinner or for a drink from time to time, from year to year. Occasional visitors assumed that it belonged to the daughter and was kept downstairs on display because it was a really fine doll's house, a regular work of art, and miniatures were coming into or recently had been in vogue. To certain rather difficult guests, including the dean of his college, the professor, without affirming or denying his part as architect, cabinetmaker, roofer, glazier, electrician, and *tapissier,* might quote Claude Lévi-Strauss. "It's in *La Pensée sauvage,* I think," he would say. "His idea is that the reduced model—the miniature—allows a knowledge of the whole to precede the knowledge of the parts. A reversal of the usual process of knowing. Essentially, all the arts proceed that way, reducing a material dimension in favor of an intellectual dimension." He found that persons entirely incapable of, and averse to, the kind of concrete thought that was his chief pleasure in working on the house went rigid as bird dogs at the name of the father of Structuralism, and sometimes continued to gaze at the doll's house for some minutes with the tense and earnest gaze of a pointer at a sitting duck. The professor's wife had to entertain a good many strangers when she became state coördinator of the conservation organisation for which she worked, but her guests, with urgent business on their mind, admired the doll's house perfunctorily if they noticed it at all.

As the daughter, Victoria, passed through the Vickie period and, at thirteen, entered upon the Tori period, her friends no longer had to be restrained or distracted from fiddling with the fittings of the little house, wearing out the fragile mechanisms, sometimes handling the furniture carelessly in their story-games with its occupants. For there was, or had been, a family living in it. Victoria at eight had requested and received for Christmas a rather expensive European mama, papa, brother, sister, and baby, all cleverly articulated so that they could sit in the armchairs, and reach up to the copper-bottom saucepans hung above the stove, and hit or clasp one another in moments of passion. Family dramas of great intensity were enacted from time to time in the then incompletely furnished house. The brother's left leg came off at the hip and was never properly mended. Papa Bendsky received a marking-pen mustache and eyebrows that gave him an evil squint, like the half-breed Lascar in an Edwardian thriller. The baby got lost. Victoria no longer played with the survivors; and the professor gratefully put them into the drawer of the table on which the house stood. He had always hated them, invaders, especially the papa, so thin, so flexible, with his nasty little Austrian-looking green jacket and his beady Lascar eyes.

Victoria had recently bought with her earnings from baby-sitting a gift to the house and her father: a china cat to drink the eternal milk from the blue bowl marked "Kitty." The professor did not put the cat in the drawer. He believed it to be worthy of the house, as the Bendsky family had never been. It was a finely modelled little figure, glazed orange and tabby on white. Curled on the hearthrug at twilight in the ruddy glow of the flames (red cellophane and a penlight bulb), it looked very comfortable indeed. But since it lay curled up, it could never go into the kitchen to drink from the blue bowl; and this was evidently a trouble or burden to the professor's unconscious mind, for he had not exactly a dream about it, one night while he was going to sleep after working late on a complex and difficult piece of writing, a response he was to give to a paper to be presented later in the year at the A.A.A.S.; not a dream, but a kind of half-waking experience. He was looking into or was in the kitchen of the inner house. That was not unusual, for when fitting the cabinets and wall panelling and building in the sink, he had become deeply familiar with the proportions and aspects of the kitchen from every angle, and had frequently and deliberately visualised it from the perspective of a six-inch person standing by the stove or at the pantry door. But in this case he had no sense of volition; he was merely there; and while standing there, near the big wood-burning stove, he saw the cat come in, look up at him, and settle itself down to drink the milk. The experience included the auditory: he heard the neat and amusing sound a cat makes lapping.

Next day he remembered this little vision clearly. His mind ran upon it, now and then. Walking across campus after a lecture, he thought with some intensity that it would be very pleasant to have an animal in the house, a live animal. Not a cat, of course. Something very small. But his precise visual imagination at once presented him with a gerbil the size of the sofa, a monstrous hamster in the master bedroom, like the dreadful Mrs. Bhoolaboy in *Staying On,* billowing in the bed, immense, and he laughed inwardly, and winced away from the spectacle.

Once, indeed, when he had been installing the pull-chain toilet—the house and its furnishings were generally Victorian; that was the original eponymous joke—he had glanced up to see that a moth had got into the attic, but only after a moment of shock did he recognise it as a moth, the marvellous, soft-winged, unearthly owl beating there beneath the rafters. Flies, however, which often visited the house, brought only thoughts of horror movies about professors who tampered with what man was not meant to know and ended up buzzing at the window pane, crying vainly, "Don't! No!" as the housewife's inexorable swatter fell. And serve them right. Would a ladybug do for a tortoise? The size was right, the colors wrong. The Victorians did not hesitate to paint live tortoise's shells. But tortoises do not raise their shells and fly away home. There was no pet suitable for the house.

Lately he had not been working much on the house; weeks and months went by before he got the tiny Landseer framed, and then it was a plain gilt frame fitted up on a Sunday afternoon, not the scrollwork masterpiece he had originally planned. Sketches for a glassed-in sun porch were never, as his dean would have put it, implemented. The personal and professional stresses in his department at the university, which had first driven him to this small escape hatch, were considerably eased under the new chairman; he and Julia had worked out their problems well enough to go on with; and anyway, the house and all its furnishings were done, in place, complete. Every armchair its antimacassars. Now that the Bendskys were gone, nothing got lost or broken, nothing even got moved. And no rain fell. The outer house was in real need of re-roofing; it had required three attic buckets this October, and even so there had been some damage to the study ceiling. But the cedar shingles on the inner house were still blond, virginal. They knew little of sunlight, and nothing of the rain.

I could, the professor thought, pour water on the roof, to weather the shingles a bit. It ought to be sprinkled on, somehow, so it would be more like rain. He saw himself stand with Julia's green plastic half-gallon watering can at the low table in the book-lined alcove of the living room; he saw water falling on the little shingles, pooling on the table, dripping to the ancient but serviceable domestic Oriental rug. He saw a mad professor watering a toy house. Will it grow, Doctor? Will it grow?

That night he dreamed that the inner house, his house, was outside. It stood in a garden patch on a rickety support of some kind. The ground around it had been partly dug up as if for planting. The sky was low and dingy, though it was not raining yet. Some slats had come away from the back of the house, and he was worried about the glue. "I'm worried about the glue," he said to the gardener or whoever it was that was there with a short-handled shovel, but the person did not understand. The house should not be outside, but it was outside, and it was too late to do anything about it.

He woke in great distress from this dream and could not find rest from it until his mind came upon the notion of, as it were, obeying the dream: actually moving the inner house outdoors, into the garden, which would then become the garden of both houses. An inner garden within the outer garden could be designed. Julia's advice would be needed for that. Miniature roses for hawthorn trees, surely. Scotch moss for the lawn? What could you use for hedges? She might know. A fountain? . . . He drifted back to sleep contentedly planning the garden of the house. And for months, even years, after that he amused or consoled himself from time to time, on troubled nights or in boring meetings, by reviving the plans for the miniature garden. But really it was not a practicable idea, given the rainy weather of his part of the world.

He and Julia got their house re-roofed eventually, and brought the buckets down from the attic. The inner house was moved upstairs into Victoria's room when she went off to college. Looking into that room towards dusk of a November evening, the professor saw the peaked roofs and widow's walk sharp against the window light. They were still dry. Dust falls here, not rain, he thought. It isn't fair. He opened the front of the house and turned on the fireplace. The little cat lay curled up on the rug before the ruddy glow, the illusion of warmth, the illusion of shelter. And the dry milk in the half-full bowl marked "Kitty" by the kitchen door. And the child gone.

RUBY ON THE 67

"I told her, I said, now don't worry about it, Jack's coming over this afternoon to put those bulbs in, you just wait till he comes. You know we had our tickets to New York? For the next morning?"

"Today?"

"Yes. No—yesterday morning it would have been. I have no idea what day it is by now!"

Anybody in the front half of the 67 bus could listen if they liked. Ruby spoke up, knowing Emma was a little deaf. Emma's grandson, a sedate man of thirty-five or so, sat silent beside her, indifferent or embarrassed, it didn't matter which. How could he understand, why should he understand?

"So I come into the dining room and there she is setting up the stepladder. I say, Rose, are you crazy? and I put it away. She goes for her nap, I'm packing my clothes for New York, I hear this awful noise, oh my God. There's Rose, the ladder, the chandelier, all over the dining room. Still holding the light bulb! Both her wrists—her big toe—one rib! Can you believe it? And for what? A light bulb. And Jack came to put them in before the ambulance got there!"

Emma's soft face as she listened expressed shock, sympathy, and stoic mockery. Emma and Ruby, never close friends, had known each other for seventy years or so.

Others were involved in the drama; a woman in her fifties sitting across the aisle shook her head and said, "Oh, oh, oh!" in a dying fall. Ruby was sitting on one of the handicapped-elderly benches behind the driver, Emma on the first front-facing seat on that side. By leaning towards Emma's neat grey head, Ruby created a little corner, the intimacy of which was not seriously disturbed by the one small doddery-looking woman sitting between them, or the fiftyish woman and the girl with grocery bags listening across the aisle, or Emma's silent grandson looking out the window.

"Johnnie was coming down from Cambridge—Ann was coming from Wellesley. All the grandkids. A regular family reunion for Thanksgiving. She's been talking about it for weeks. But I tell you I felt it in my bones that it wasn't to be. You know she's only been out of hospital a week with that bronchitis. And airports. And cold, it's cold out there in the East! Terrible winters they have. The airplanes freeze to the ground. I thought, this is not to be. Something will happen. But this!"

"Your mother?" asked the woman across the aisle.

"My sister. Eighty-three," Ruby answered with cordial dignity, and turned again to Emma, who was saying, "There was something they used to say when something like this—what's the Yiddish, remember, what your father always said—"

"I know, I know! I can't remember." Emma and Ruby both laughed, and Ruby said, "All going, it's all going."

"Where is she in hospital?"

"Oh, I brought her home last night. What can they do I can't? She's all right, just can't do a thing, nothing. Bertha's with her so I could get to the bank. I'd planned to go that afternoon. I had a dollar and eight pennies, imagine."

"Both hands? And her leg, you said?"

"Both wrists. So she can't do a thing for herself. And her big toe, and a rib in back, it got cracked where it comes around in back, the way she fell. Oh, and is she fussy. She doesn't want me to sponge bathe her." Ruby leaned forward across the intervening small woman so that she could lower her voice to talk about such matters. "Me! Her sister! From the same mother born! What is she thinking of? Crazy. Rose has always been crazy, you know."

Emma laughed again and clicked her tongue. She said with warmth, "Poor Meyer! What a fine man he was."

"He was."

"I only know widows any more."

"Is there anybody else? But you have your children living here in town, you're lucky, Emma."

"Hospital's the next stop," Emma's grandson said, and Emma obediently buttoned the top button of her coat and got a grip on her handbag. "I'm seeing Suzy, she's in with the emphysema. You know Suzy Wise, Ruby. Norman Wise's wife. He died last year. Listen." The bus slowed for the stop by the stuccoed bulk of the hospital, and Emma stood, holding on to the vertical post. She said, "Keep your chin up, Ruby. It feels better up."

"I do, sure. So take care, both of you!"

The small woman next to Ruby was nodding in a quivery but vigorous way. The fiftyish one across the aisle smiled, and the young one with grocery sacks was gazing intently. As Emma made her way to the steps and slowly descended them, watched from the pavement by her impassive grandson, the whole front end of the bus was briefly charged with the dry warmth of approval. A heavy elderly man on Ruby's right, who had got on at some time during her conversation, made a noise in his throat, a kind of "Hah!" as if he were speaking to them all but did not have words to speak with.

Six stops later Ruby got off, also slowly, favoring the repair-job hip. The heavy man followed her and turned away, waiting for the light. She walked up the hill carefully. The November air was mild and wet, the pavement slick with old leaves. No good falling down on the job now, my God. She thought of Emma's steady little voice and nodded, agreeing with her. And even now she could carry her height well. She always had. A good carriage, Grandfather had used to say. As a little kid she had thought he meant horses and a buggy. Young women now didn't think much about how they carried themselves, but it mattered. Rose, Rose as a young woman, walking, what a beauty! Both of them, before they married, for that matter. At twenty-two and eighteen, Rose and Ruby, my God! Keeping up all that so long, and the streets all changed, the old house gone. She walked on, carefully, chin up, carrying through the grey air her head crowned with hair dyed, for the last forty years, a light, soft red.

LIMBERLOST

The poet revolved slowly counterclockwise in the small, dark, not very deep pool. The novelist sat on the alder log that dammed the creek to make the pool. Also on the log were the poet's clothes, except his underpants. Coming upstream to the swimming hole they had passed a naked nut-brown maid, beached and frontal to the sun; but she was young and they were not; and the poet was not Californian. "You don't mind if I'm old-fashioned about modesty?" he had asked, disarmingly. The novelist, although a Californian, did not mind. The poet's massive body was impressive enough as it was. Age, slacking here and tightening there what had been all smooth evenness in youth, gave pathos and dignity to that strong beast turning in the dark water. Among roots and the dark shadows of the banks, the hands and arms shone white. The novelist's bare feet, though tanned, also gleamed pallid under the water, as she sat rather less than comfortably on the log wondering whether she should have pulled off shirt and jeans and joined the poet in his pool. She had been at his Conference less than an hour and did not know the rules. Did he want a companion, or a spectator? Did it matter? She splashed the water with her feet and deplored her inability to do, to know, what she wanted herself—fifty-five years old and sitting in adolescent paralysis, a bump on a log. Should I swim? I don't want to. I want to. Should I? Which underpants am I wearing? This is like the first day of summer camp. I want to go home. I ought to swim. Ought I? Now?

The poet spared her further debate by hauling out on the far end of the log. He was shivering. The log was in sunlight, but the air was cool. Discovering that he would not soon get dry in wet boxer shorts, he did then remove them, but very modestly, back turned, sitting down again quickly. He spread his underpants out on the log to dry, and conversed with his guest.

An expansive gesture as he described the events of the first week of the Conference swept his socks into the water. He caught one, but the current took the other out of reach. It sank slowly. He mourned; the novelist commiserated. He dismissed the sock.

"The Men have raised a Great Phallus farther up the river," he said, smiling. "It was their own idea. I'd show you, but it's off limits to the Women. A temenos. Very interesting, some of the ritual that has developed this week! I am hearing men talk—not sports scores and business, but talk—"

Impressed and interested, the novelist listened, trying to ignore a lesser fascination: the sock. It had re-emerged, all the way across the sun-flecked water, under a muddy, rooty bank. It was now moving very slowly but apparently—yes—definitely clock-wise in a circle that would bring it back towards the log. The novelist sought and found a broken branch and held it ready, idly teasing the water with it. Housewife, she thought, ashamed. Fixated on socks. Prose-writer!

The poet, sensitive and alert even when talking of his concerns, observed, and asked what she was fishing for.

"Your sock is coming back," she said.

In a silence of complete fellow-feeling they both watched the stately progress of the floating sock, coming round unhurried in the fullness of time, astronomically certain, till the current brought it within branch-reach. It was lifted dripping on the forked end. In quiet triumph the novelist turned the branch to the poet, presenting the sock to its owner, who removed it from the branch and squeezed it thoughtfully.

Soon after this he dressed; and they returned downstream to the Conference center and the scattered cabins under the redwoods.

The food was marvelous. Infinitely imaginatively vegetarian, eclectic but not hodgepodge: the chilis hot, the salads delicate, the curries fragrant. The kitchen staff who produced these wonders were unlike the other people at the Conference, though in fact several of them were members of the Conference working out their fees. When they came out front and listened to the lecture on The Hero they disappeared into the others, she could not recognise them; but in the crowded, hot, flashing kitchen each of them seemed almost formidably individual, laughing more than anyone else here, talking differently, moving with deft purpose, so that the onlooker felt superfluous and inferior, not because the cooks meant to impress or to exclude but only because, being busy with the work in hand, they were quite unconscious of doing so.

After dinner on the second day, in honey-colored evening sunlight, crossing the broad wooden bridge across the creek between the main hall and her group of cabins, the novelist stopped and set her hands on the rough railing. "I have been here before! I know this creek, this bridge, that trail going up into the trees—" Such moments were a familiar accompaniment to tension and self-consciousness. She had felt them while waiting to be asked to dance in dancing class at twelve, and at fifty in a hotel room in a city she had never seen before. Sometimes they justified themselves as a foresight remembered, bringing with them a queer double-exposure effect of that place where she had foreseen being in this place. But this time the experience was one of pure recognition, unexplainable but not uncanny, though solemnified by the extraordinary grandeur of the setting.

For the creek ran and the path led from fog-softened golden light into a darkness under incredible trees. It was always dark under them, and silent, and bare, for their huge community admitted little on a smaller scale. In the open clearings weeds and brambles and birds and bugs made the usual lively mess and tangle; under the big trees the flash of a scrub jay's wing startled as it would in the austere reaches of a Romanesque church. To come under the trees was as definite a transition as entering a building, but a building the size of a county.

Yet in among those immense living trunks there were also some black, buttressed objects which confused the sense of scale still further, for though squat, they were bigger than the cabins—much bigger. In bulk and girth, they were bigger than the trees. They were ruins. Tree ruins, the logged and burned-over stumps of the original forest. With effort, the novelist comprehended that the sequoias so majestically towering their taper bulk and gracile limbs all around here were second growth, not even a century old, mere saplings, shoots, scions of the great presences that had grown here in a length of silence now altogether and forever lost.

All the same, it was very quiet under the trees, and still quieter at night. There were refinements of the absence of sound which the novelist had never before had the opportunity to observe. The cabins of her group straggled along, one every ten or twenty yards, unlighted, above the creek, which ran shallow but almost soundless, as if obeying the authority of the redwoods, their counsel of silence. There was no wind. Fog would mosey in over the hills from the sea before dawn to hush what was hushed already. Far away one small owl called once. Later, one mosquito shrilled hopelessly for a moment at the screen.

The novelist lay in darkness on her narrow board bunk in her sleeping bag listening to nothing and wondering if this was the bag her daughter had been using when she got the flu camping last summer and how long flu germs might live in the dark, warm, moist medium of a zippered sleeping bag. Her thoughts ran on such matters because she was acutely uncomfortable. Sometimes she thought it was diarrhea, sometimes a bladder infection, sometimes a coward spirit. Whatever it was, would it force her yet again to leave the germy warmth of the sleeping bag and take her flashlight and try to find the evasive path up that ominous hill to the all too communal, doorless, wet-floored toilets, praying that nobody would join her in her misery? Yes. No, maybe not. She heard a screen door creak, a cabin or two downstream, and almost immediately after, a soft, rushing noise: a man pissing off his cabin porch onto the dark, soft, absorbent ground of redwood leaf and twig and bark. O lucky Men, who need not crouch and straddle! Her bladder twinged, remorseless. "I do not have to go pee," she told herself, unconvinced. "I am not sick." She listened to the terrific silence. Nothing lived. But there, deep in the hollow darkness, a soft, lively sound: a little fart. And, now that she was all ears, presently another fart, louder, from a cabin on higher ground. The beans with chilis would probably explain it. Or did it need explanation, did people like cattle add nightly to the methane in the atmosphere, had those who had slept in longhouses by this creek been accustomed to this soft concert? For it was pleasing, almost melodious, this sparse pattern of a snore here—a long efflatus there—a little sigh—against the black and utter stillness.

When she was nearly asleep, she heard voices far upstream, male voices, chanting, as if from the dawn of history. Deep, primeval. The Men were performing the rituals of manhood. But the little farts in the night were nearer and dearer.

The Women sat in a circle on the sand, about thirty of them. Nearby the shallow river widened to the sea. Soft, fog-paled sunshine of the north coast lay beautifully on low breakers and dunes. The Women passed an ornamented wooden wand from hand to hand; who held the wand spoke; the others listened. It did not seem quite right to the novelist. A good thing, but not the right one. Men wanted wands, women did not, she thought. These women had dutifully accepted the wand, but left to themselves they might have preferred some handwork and sat talking round and about like a flock of sparrows. Sparrows are disorderly, don't take turns, don't shut up to listen to the one with the wand, peck and talk at the same time. The wind blew softly, the wand passed. A woman in her twenties who wore an emblem of carved wood and feathers on a chain round her neck read a manuscript poem in a trembling voice half lost in the distant sound of the breakers. "My arms are those wings," she read, her voice shaken by fear and passion till it broke. The wand passed. A blonde, fine-boned woman in her forties spoke of the White Goddess, but the novelist had ceased to listen, nervously rehearsing what she would say, should she say it? should she not? The wand passed to her. "It seems to me, coming in from outside, into the middle of this, you know, just for a couple of days, but perhaps just because of that I can be useful, anyhow it seems to me that to some extent some of the women here are sort of looking for a, for something actually to sort of *do*. Instead of kind of talking mostly in a sort of derivative way," she said in a harsh, chirping voice like a sparrow's. Shaking, she passed the wand. After the circle broke up, several women told her with enthusiasm about the masked dancing last Wednesday night, when the Women had acted out the female archetype of their choice. "It got wild," one said cheerfully. Another woman told her that this leader of the Women had quarreled with that one and personalities were destroying harmony. Several of them started making a large dragon out of wet sand, and while doing so told her that this year was different from earlier years, before the Men and the Women were separated, and that the East Coast meetings were always more spiritual than the West Coast meetings, or vice versa. They all chattered till the Men came back from their part of the beach, some with faces marked splendidly with charcoal.

The fine-boned blonde whom the novelist had not listened to

rode beside her in the car going back inland, a long, rough road through the logged-out Coast Range. "I've been coming to this place all my life," she said with a laugh. "It was a summer camp. I started coming when I was ten. Oh, it was wonderful then! I still meet people who came to Limberlost."

"Limberlost!" said the novelist.

"It was Camp Limberlost," said the other woman, and laughed again, affectionately.

"But I went there," said the novelist. "I went to Camp Limberlost. You mean this is it? Where the Conference is? But I was wondering, earlier this year, I realised I had no idea where it was, or how to find out. I didn't know where it was when I went there. It was in the redwoods, that's literally all I knew. We all got into a bus downtown, and talked for six hours, you know, and then we were there—you know how kids are, they don't *notice*. But it was a Girl Reserve camp then. The YW ran it. I had to join the Girl Reserves to come."

"The city took it over after the war," the other woman said, her eyes merry and knowing. "This really is it. This is Limberlost."

"But I don't remember it," the novelist said in distress.

"The Conference is in the old Boys Camp. The Girls Camp was upstream about a mile. Maybe you never came down here."

Yes. The novelist remembered that Jan and Dorothy had cut Campfire one evening and sneaked out of camp and down the creek to Boys Camp. They had hidden across the creek behind stumps and shrubs in the twilight, they had hooted and bleated and meowed until the Boys began coming out of their cabins, and then a counsellor had come out, and Jan and Dorothy had run away, and got back after dark, muddy and triumphant, madly giggling in the jammed cabin after Lights Out, reciting their adventure, counting coup. . . .

But she had not gone with them. There was no way she could have remembered that bridge across the creek, the trail going up out of the evening light.

Still, how could she not have recognised the place as a whole—the forest, the cabins? Two weeks of three summers she had lived here, at twelve and thirteen and fourteen, and had she never noticed the silence? the size of the redwoods? the black, appalling, giant stumps?

It was forty years; the trees might have grown a good deal—and now, as she thought, it did seem that she and Jan had actually climbed one of the stumps one day to sit and talk, cutting Crafts, probably. But they hadn't thought anything about the stump but that it was climbable, a place to talk in privacy. No sense of what that huge wreck meant, except (like those who had cut the tree) to their own convenience; no notion of what it was in relation to anything else, or where it was, or where they were. They were here. Despairingly homesick the first night, thereafter settled in. At home in the world, as cheekily indifferent to cause and effect as sparrows, as ignorant of death and geography as the redwoods.

She had envied Jan and Dorothy their exploit, knowing them to be a good deal braver than she was. They had agreed to take her back to Boys Camp with them, and hoot and meow, or just hide and watch, but they never got around to it. They all went to Campfire and sang lonesome cowboy songs instead. So she had never seen Boys Camp until she came here and sat on the log and watched the poet circle slowly in the pool, and what would she and Jan and Dorothy, fourteen, merciless, have thought of *that*? "Oh, Lord!" she said involuntarily.

The woman beside her in the car laughed, as if in sympathy. "It's such a beautiful place," she said, "it's wonderful to be able to come back. What do you think of the Conference?"

"I like the drumming," the novelist replied, after a pause, with fervor. "The drumming is wonderful. I never did that before." Indeed she had found that she wanted to do nothing else. If only there weren't a lecture tonight and they could drum again after dinner, thirty or forty people each with a drum on or between their knees, the rhythm set and led by a couple of drummers who knew what they were doing and kept the easy yet complex beat and pattern going, going, going till there was nothing in consciousness but that and nothing else needed, no words at all.

The lecture was on the Wild Man. That night she woke up in the pitch dark and went out without using her flashlight and pissed beside her cabin, almost noiselessly. She heard no local breaking of wind, but guessed that many of the cabins were still empty; the Men had all gone off upstream, off limits, after the lecture, and now she heard them not chanting but yelling and roaring, a wild noise, but so far away that it didn't make much of a dent on the silence here. Here at Limberlost.

In the low, cold mist of morning the poet came from cabin to cabin. The novelist heard him coming, chanting and making animal sounds, banging the screen doors of the cabins. He wore a dramatic animal mask, a grey, snarling, hairy snout. "Up! Up! Daybreak! The old wolf's at the door! The wolf, the wolf!" he chanted, entering a cabin in a predatory crouch. Sleepy voices protested laughingly. The novelist was already up and dressed and had performed t'ai chi. She had stayed inside the screened cabin instead of going out on its spacious porch, because she was self-conscious, because doing t'ai chi was just too damn much the kind of thing you did here and yet didn't fit at all with what they were doing here, and anyhow she was going home today and would damn well do t'ai chi in the broom closet if that's where she felt like doing it.

The poet approached her cabin and paused. "Good morning!" he said politely and incongruously through his staring, hairy muzzle. "Good morning," said the novelist from behind her screens, feeling a surge of snobbish irritation at the silly poet parading his power to wake everybody up, but *she* was up already!—and at the same time yearning to be able to go out and pat the wolf, to call him brave, to play the game he wanted so much to play, or at least to offer him something better than a wet sock on a stick.

THE CREATURES ON MY MIND

THE BEETLE

When I stayed for a week in New Orleans, out near Tulane, I had an apartment with a balcony. It wasn't one of those cast-iron-lace showpieces of the French Quarter, but a deep, wood-railed balcony made for sitting outside in privacy, just the kind of place I like. But when I first stepped out on it, the first thing I saw was a huge beetle. It lay on its back directly under the light fixture. I thought it was dead, then saw its legs twitch and twitch again. No doubt it had been attracted by the light the night before, and had flown into it, and damaged itself mortally.

Big insects horrify me. As a child I feared moths and spiders, but adolescence cured me, as if those fears evaporated in the stew of hormones. But I never got enough hormones to make me easy with the large, hard-shelled insects: wood roaches, june bugs, mantises, cicadas. This beetle was a couple of inches long; its abdomen was ribbed, its legs long and jointed; it was dull reddish-brown; it was dying. I felt a little sick seeing it lie there twitching, enough to keep me from sitting out on the balcony that first day.

61

Next morning, ashamed of my queasiness, I went out with the broom to sweep it away. But it was still twitching its legs and antennae, still dying. With the end of the broom handle I pushed it very gently a little farther towards the corner of the balcony, and then I sat to read and make notes in the wicker chair in the other corner, turned away from the beetle, because its movements drew my eyes. My intense consciousness of it seemed to have something to do with my strangeness in that strange city, New Orleans, and my sense of being on the edge of the tropics, a hot, damp, swarming, fetid, luxuriant existence, as if my unease took the beetle as its visible sign. Why else did I think of it so much? I weighed maybe two thousand times what it weighed, and lived in a perceptual world utterly alien from its world. My feelings were quite out of proportion.

And if I had any courage or common sense, I kept telling myself, I'd step on the poor damned creature and put it out of its misery. We don't know what a beetle may or may not suffer, but it was, in the proper sense of the word, in agony, and the agony had gone on two nights and two days now. I put on my leather-soled loafers; but then I couldn't step on it. It would crunch, ooze, squirt under my shoe. Could I hit it with the broom handle? No, I couldn't. I have had a cat with leukemia put down, and have stayed with a cat while he died; I think that if I was hungry, if I had reason to, I could kill for food, wring a chicken's neck, as my grandmothers did, with no more guilt and no less fellow-feeling than they. My inability to kill this creature had nothing ethical about it, and no kindness in it. It was mere squeamishness. It was a little rotten place in me, like the soft brown spots in fruit: a sympathy that came not from respect, but from loathing. It was a responsibility that would not act. It was guilt itself.

On the third morning the beetle was motionless, shrunken, dead. I got the broom again and swept it into the gutter of the balcony among dry leaves. And there it still is in the gutter of my mind among dry leaves, a tiny dry husk, a ghost.

THE SPARROW

In the humid New England summer the little cooling plant ran all day, making a deep, loud noise. Around the throbbing machinery was a frame of coarse wire net. I thought the bird was outside that wire net, then I hoped it was, then I wished it was. It was moving back and forth with the regularity of the trapped, the zoo animal that paces twelve feet east and twelve feet west and twelve feet east and twelve feet west, hour after hour; the heartbeat of the prisoner in the cell before the torture; the unending recurrence, the silent, steady panic. Back and forth steadily fluttering between two wooden uprights just above a beam that supported the wire screen: a sparrow, an ordinary sparrow, dusty, scrappy. I've seen sparrows fighting over territory till the feathers fly, and fucking cheerfully on telephone wires, and in winter they gather in trees in crowds like dirty little Christmas ornaments and talk all together like noisy children, chirp, charp, chirp, charp! But this sparrow was alone, and back and forth it went in terrible silence, trapped in wire and fear. What could I do? There was a door to the wire cage, but it was padlocked. I went on. I tell you I felt that bird beat its wings right here, here under my breastbone in the hollow of my heart. I said in my mind, Is it my fault? Did I build the cage? Just because I happened to see it, is it my sparrow? But my heart was low already, and I knew now that I would be down, down like a bird whose wings won't bear it up, a starving bird.

Then on the path I saw the man, one of the campus managers. The bird's fear gave me courage to speak. "I'm so sorry to bother you," I said. "I'm just visiting here at the Librarians Conference, we met the other day in the office. I didn't know what to do, because there's a bird that got into the cooling plant there, inside the screen, and it can't get out." That was enough, too much, but I had to go on. "The noise of the machinery, I think the noise confuses it, and I didn't know what to do. I'm sorry." Why did I apologise? For what?

"Have a look," he said, not smiling not frowning.

He turned and came with me. He saw the bird beating back and forth, back and forth in silence. He unlocked the padlock. He had the key.

The bird didn't see the door open behind it. It kept beating back and forth along the screen. I found a little stick on the path and threw it against the outside of the screen to frighten the bird into breaking its pattern. It went the wrong way, deeper into the cage, towards the machinery. I threw another stick, hard, and the bird veered and then turned and flew out. I watched the open door, I saw it fly.

The man and I closed the door. He locked it. "Be getting on," he said, not smiling not frowning, and went on his way, a manager with a lot on his mind, a hardworking man. But did he have no joy of it? That's what I think about now. Did he have the key, the power to set free, the will to do it, but no joy in doing it? It is his soul I think about now, if that is the word for it, the spirit, that sparrow.

THE GULL

They were winged, all the creatures on my mind.

This one is hard to tell about. It was a seagull. Gulls on Klatsand beach, on any North Pacific shore, are all alike in their two kinds: white adults with black wingtips and yellow bills, and young gulls, adult-sized but with delicately figured brown feathers. They soar and cry, swoop, glide, dive, squabble and grab; they stand in their multitudes at evening in the sunset shallows of the creek mouth before they rise in silence to fly out to sea, where they will sleep the night afloat on waves far out beyond the breakers, like a fleet of small white ships with sails furled and no riding lights. Gulls eat anything, gulls clean the beach, gulls eat dead gulls. There are no individual gulls. They are magnificent flyers, big, clean, strong birds, rapacious, suspicious, fearless. Sometimes as they ride the wind I have seen them as part of the wind and the sea exactly as the foam, the sand, the fog is part of it all, all one, and in such moments of vision I have truly seen the gulls.

But this was one gull, an individual, for it stood alone near the low-tide water's edge with a broken wing. I saw first that the left wing dragged, then saw the naked bone jutting like an ivory knife up from blood-rusted feathers. Something had attacked it, something that could half tear away a wing, maybe a shark when it dove to catch a fish. It stood there. As I came nearer, it saw me. It gave no sign. It did not sidle away, as gulls do when you walk towards them, and then fly if you keep coming on. I stopped. It stood, its flat red feet in the shallow water of a tidal lagoon above the breakers. The tide was on the turn, returning. It stood and waited for the sea.

The idea that worried me was that a dog might find it before the sea did. Dogs roam that long beach. A dog chases gulls, barking and rushing, excited; the gulls fly up in a rush of wings; the dog trots back, maybe a little hangdog, to its owner strolling far down the beach. But a gull that could not fly and the smell of blood would put a dog into a frenzy of barking, lunging, teasing, torturing. I imagined that. My imagination makes me human and makes me a fool, it gives me all the world and exiles me from it. The gull stood waiting for the dog, for the other gulls, for the tide, for what came, living its life completely until death. Its eyes look straight through me, seeing truly, seeing nothing but the sea, the sand, the wind.

STANDING GROUND

They were coming: two of them. The trembling began in Mary's fingertips and ran up her arms into her heart. She must stand her ground. Mr. Young had said stand your ground. He might come. If he came, they would never get past him. She wished Norman would not shake his sign like that. The shaking made the trembling worse. The sign was something Norman had made himself, not one Mr. Young had approved, even. Norman had no right to do everything himself that way. This is a war, Mr. Young said, and we are the army of the Right. We are soldiers. They were coming closer, and the trembling ran down into her legs, but she stood firm, she stood her ground.

An old man standing on the sidewalk ahead of them was holding up a sign on a stick, and when he saw them he began to shake it up and down. It had some dark words on it and a picture of what looked like a possum. "What's that?" Sharee asked, and Delaware said, "Road kill." There was a woman, too, almost hidden by the man's sign. Delaware thought she might be an escort. She was calling out to them. Sharee asked, "Who's she?" and Delaware said, "I don't know, come on," because the man was making her nervous. He had started making a kind of chopping motion with the sign, as if he was going to cut them down with the dead possum. The woman was pretty and nicely dressed, but instead of talking softer as they came close she yelled louder: "I'm praying! I'm praying for you!" "Why doesn't she go to church?" Sharee asked. She and Delaware were holding hands now, and they walked faster. The woman danced in front of them like a basketball player trying to stop a shot. Her voice had gone up into a scream, shrill, in Sharee's face: "Mom, Mom! Stop her! Stop her, Mom!" To shut out the screaming woman Sharee put her free arm up over her eyes and ducked her head down between her shoulders as they hurried up the four steps of the building. The man was also shouting now. Delaware felt the edge of his signboard strike her shoulder, a terrible feeling, not a pain but a shock, an invasion. It seemed like she had expected it, had known it would happen, but it was so terrible it stopped her and she could not move. Sharee tugged her forward to the metal-framed pebble-glass door of the clinic and pushed at the door. It did not move. Delaware thought it was locked and they were trapped, outside. The door opened outward fast, forcing them back. An angry woman stood there saying, "There's an injunction against you getting on this property and you'd better not forget it!" Sharee let go Delaware's hand and ducked way down and hid her head in both arms. Delaware looked around and saw where the angry woman was looking. "She's talking to them," she said to Sharee. "It's OK." She took Sharee's hand again, and they went inside, past the angry woman, who held the door for them.

They were in there now. They had got in. And Pitch Defilement was laughing at him inside the door, standing there laughing. Mary was talking in her squealy voice. Screaming and squealing and devil laughter. Norman raised up his sign and swung it down, driving it edgewise into the grass along the sidewalk in front of the Butcher Shop. Squealy Mary jumped aside and stood staring at him. He pulled the sign out and stood it upright. He felt better. "I'm going for a cup of coffee," he told Mary. Walking to the coffee shop, five blocks, carrying his sign erect, he thought all the time of what was going on inside the Butcher Shop. How they laid the girl down and gassed her and spread her legs and reached inside and found him and pried and pulled him out with the instruments. Stuck them into her, farther and farther in, grasped and pulled him out quivering and bloody. Stuck the knives up in between her legs and she writhed and moaned, showing her teeth, arching her back, gasping, panting. They pulled him out and he lay limp and little, dead. "God is my witness," he said aloud, and struck the stick of his sign against the pavement. He would find a way in. He would get in there and do what must be done.

The fat woman was behind the counter at the coffee shop. Young but fat, flaunting white, freckled arms. He didn't like the place but it was the only place to get coffee near the clinic. Lists of stuff with foreign names stood on the counter. People in expensive clothes came in and ordered the foreign names. Norman said, "I want a cup of plain American coffee," as he always did, and Lard Arms nodded. When he made the sign and started bringing it into the coffee shop, she had stopped speaking to him or smiling, and looked at him warily. That was how he wanted it. She put the filled cup on the counter. He put down exact change, took the cup to a table by the window, propping his sign up against the glass, and sat down. He felt tired. His hip hurt again, the grinding ache, and the coffee tasted weak and bitter. He stared at his sign. A long, curling hair, caught in the rough wooden edge, shimmered bright as gold wire in the sunlight coming through the glass. He reached out to pull it off. He could not feel it between his fingers, stiff and half numbed from carrying the sign all morning.

They went in front of the reception desk and the angry woman went behind it. She said to Delaware, "You're Sharee."

"I'm Sharee," Sharee said.

"It's for her," Delaware said. She moved her head and shoulders, moved forward a little, to get the receptionist to look at her instead of at her mother. "I made the appointments for her. She saw Dr. Rourke."

The receptionist looked from one to the other. After a while she said, "Which one of you is pregnant?"

"Her," Delaware said, holding Sharee's hand.

"Me," Sharee said, holding Delaware's hand.

"Then she's Sharee Aske? Who are you?"

"Delaware Aske."

After a moment of silence, the receptionist, whose name tag said she was Kathryn, accepted that and turned to Sharee. "OK, now there's one more form to sign," she said with professional firmness, "and you for sure didn't eat anything this morning, did you?" Sharee responded at once to the institutional tone. "No," she said, shaking her head. "And I can sign the form to sign."

Delaware saw but did not acknowledge the receptionist's sudden, understanding glance at her. It was her turn to be mad. "How come you let those people yell at us out there?" she asked in an abrupt, trembling voice.

"There isn't anything we can do," the receptionist said. "They can't come onto the property. The sidewalk's free, you know." Her voice was cool.

"I thought there were escorts."

"The volunteers usually come Tuesdays, that's the regular day. Dr. Rourke put you in today because he's going on vacation. Right there, see, honey?" She showed Sharee where to sign.

"Are they going to be there when we go out?"

"Where's your car?"

"We came on the bus."

Kathryn frowned. After a pause she said, "You ought to have a taxi going home."

Delaware had no idea what it cost to ride in a taxi. She had eleven dollars and Sharee probably had around ten dollars in her bag. Maybe they could ride the taxi part way. She said nothing.

"You can call it from here. Tell it to come to the back entrance, the doctors' parking lot. OK, that's it. If you'll just sit down over there, Nurse will be with you in a minute." Kathryn gathered up the papers and went into some inner office.

"Come on," Delaware said, and went over to the sofa, two chairs, table-with-magazines arrangement. Sharee did not follow her for a while, but stood at the reception desk, looking around. Delaware still felt angry. "Come on!" she said.

Sharee came over, sat down on the sofa, and looked around from there. She had dressed for the occasion in her new jeans skirt, white cowboy boots, and blue satin cowboy jacket. Debi at the Head Shop had given her a wet-look curl in Daffodil Gold a week ago; sometimes she let it get too tangled up, but this morning it looked good, like a lion's golden mane, wild and full. Fear and excitement made her dark eyes shine. Looking at her, Delaware felt strange and sad. She picked up a magazine and stared at it.

It was a kind of pretty place. The sofa and chairs were aqua, her favorite color. Delaware was staring at a magazine and looking mad. Sometimes Delaware acted like she knew everything. She knew a lot but she wasn't the mama, she wasn't a mama at all. That was a thing she didn't know. And Sharee did know. She remembered all of it, how she stuck out in front like a piano and had to pee all the time, and how her own mama had been so mad. Mama was always mad. It was a lot easier ever since she went to Alaska with David, it was a lot easier without her, just Sharee and Delaware in the apartment, like it was meant to be. She remembered Delaware right from the first. That deep, deep softness and so small, like everything good in the world there where you could hold it and hug onto it and the milk came and it felt so good you didn't know if you were the baby or the baby was you. Delaware didn't remember that. But she did.

This time she had known right away, next morning. With Delaware she hadn't known because she wasn't thinking about babies then, she wasn't a mama, she was just thinking all the time about Donny and loving him. Then when she started sticking out in front and her mama asked her about her periods, she and Donny had broken up and she was going with Roddy. And then her mama had got so mad and she had to stop going with Roddy or anybody. But this time, this was different. This time she was mad herself. She and Donny had been in love. But this was different. What Mac did, in the car, at the drive-in, like that, like some zoo monkey, and then made her watch the rest of the movie. When he finally brought her home she took a long shower, and in the shower she thought, something's happening. Next morning, she thought, something's happening. And then when her period didn't start she knew. She knew it wouldn't. And she was really mad. People thought she never got mad, but she did. It was like it started right there in her stomach, the same place, and spread out around her like a ball of hot red light. She didn't say, but she knew. She didn't know everything but she knew what was hers. What was inside her was hers. Mac had bent her arm and covered her mouth and stuck his thing into her just like some zoo monkey, but what happened inside her was hers, and she made it happen or not happen. Delaware had happened because she was hers, her own, she made her happen. This was different. This was a piece of her like a wart, like a scab you pick off. Like Mac had hurt her, cut her, made this wound inside her. There was a scab over the wound, and she was going to get it off and be whole. She wasn't some zoo monkey or some kind of wound, she was the person she was. That was what Linda always said when she was in the special class. Be the person you are, Sharee. You are a whole person, a lovely person. And you have a lovely daughter. Aren't you proud of her? You're a good mother, Sharee. I know, Sharee always said to Linda, and she said it in her head now. Sometimes Delaware thought she was the mama, but she wasn't. Sharee was. As soon as she said she wanted the abortion, Delaware got mad-looking and bossy and kept saying are you sure, are you sure, and Sharee couldn't explain to her why she was sure. You have to be a mama to understand, she said. Sometimes I think I am, Delaware said. Sharee knew what she meant. But that wasn't the kind of mama she meant. See, you were me until you were you, she told Delaware. I did you. I made you be. But this one isn't like that. It isn't me, it's just like this wrong piece of me I don't want, like a hangnail. Jeez, Mama! Delaware said, and Sharee told her don't swear. Anyway, Delaware knew she knew what she was doing, and stopped asking are you sure, and got the appointment with Dr. Rourke. Now she was sitting on the aqua sofa looking sad again. Sharee took her hand. "You are my Knight in Shining Armor," she said. Delaware looked really surprised and then said, "Oh, jeez, Mama," but not mad. "Don't swear," Sharee said.

A nurse came in from the hall, a white woman in nurses' ugly pale green slacks and smock. She looked at them both and smiled. "Hi!" she said.

"Hi!" Sharee said, and smiled.

The nurse looked at the papers in her hand. "OK, just checking," she said. "You're Sharee," she said to Delaware. "How old are you, Sharee?"

"Thirty-one," Sharee said.

"Right. And how old are you, honey?"

"I just came here with her," Delaware said.

"Yeah," the nurse said, looking confused. She stared at the papers and then at Delaware. "Then it isn't you that's here for the procedure?"

Delaware shook her head.

"But we need to know your age."

"What for?"

The nurse went official. "Are you a minor?"

"Yes," Delaware said, nasty.

73

The nurse turned and went off without saying anything.

Sharee picked up a magazine with Kevin Costner on the cover. "That man looks mad," she said, studying the photograph. "There's a man comes into the Frosty that looks mad like that all the time. He's really cute, though. He always gets the burger no fries and a strawberry softie. I don't like softies. They don't taste like anything. I like the hard ice cream. The old fashion. Old fashion hard ice cream. That's what you like too, isn't it?"

Delaware nodded, and then said, "Yes," because Sharee needed you to say things. She had found that she wanted to cry, that is, that she was ready to cry but didn't want to. The cause was the place on her shoulder where the man's sign had hit her. She wanted to cry because it hurt. She wasn't hurt. There was no mark on her jeans jacket. There would be nothing but a little bruise on her, something she'd see tonight when she undressed, or maybe nothing. But the place where the wooden edge of the sign had hit felt separately alive and hurtful. It made her heart cold and her throat swollen. She took deep breaths. The nurse came back.

"OK, honey!" she said to the air between Sharee and Delaware.

Sharee jumped right up, her turn to dance. She got hold of Delaware's hand and tugged her up. "Come on!" she said, looking excited and pretty.

Norman had no right to just walk off like that. He was rude and selfish. His sign had not hit the girl in the shoulder, but if it had, if it had happened to, it could quite well have gotten both of them into trouble again. He had absolutely no right to do that. Swinging the sign around that way. He could have hit her. He had no right. He never obeyed orders. She would have to tell Mr. Young if Norman was so unreliable.

It was past nine and no one else would be coming. She looked down the block, but there was no one on foot, and none of the cars that came by slowed down. That terrible woman in her boots and a satin jacket like some circus performer, dragging the girl, her own daughter, you could see how alike they looked. That poor girl, she should pray for her. Only she was so angry, it was hard to pray. She could pray for the baby. And the father. Some poor boy, maybe a serviceman, a soldier, and no doubt he didn't even know, what did they care about *his* rights, nothing. Nothing but self, self, self. They had no right. They were animals.

Her throat was sore and her hands were trembling again. She hated it when her hands trembled. They said soldiers were afraid on the battlefield. But the trembling made her feel that she was like Grandpa Kevory sitting in the dark room that smelled of urine, his big, white hands trembling and shaking, you'll have to help me hold that cup, Mary, and then his head would jerk, on purpose, and the water would run down his chin and he would shake Mary with his horrible shaking hands. No one would come.

They had no right to expect her to stand here alone. Norman was supposed to be here. He had volunteered. She had only come because she had missed last Tuesday because she had to substitute for the secretary at the school and always made up for time she missed. She had promised Mr. Young. Promises were important to her. No one else really cared. They came when they felt like it and never thought a thing about not being there if it was the least bit inconvenient for them. He had no right to walk off like that, leaving her alone without a sign or anything, thinking of nothing but himself. She had thought that maybe Mr. Young would happen to drive by and see her standing there keeping guard, keeping the faith, but there were no cars coming down the street. No one was coming. No one would come.

I am a soldier, she thought, and as always the thought moved through her making her strong. The brave boys were there defending the flag: she saw the flag waving bright and clean over clouds of oily blackness. She would ask Mr. Young if she could carry an American flag when she was on duty. American flags were on sale now at the mall, with yellow bows. I am a soldier of

Life. I am on guard. She stood straight and walked up and down the sidewalk in front of the clinic, turning on her heel at the end of the lawn. She was glad and proud to be a soldier.

Going down the hall, Delaware said to the nurse, "Can I come in?" But she had blown it not saying how old she was. The nurse walked right on and said, "Ask Doctor," in an eat-shit voice.

Why did they talk baby talk, anyhow, wait for Nurse, ask Doctor?

Dr. Rourke greeted her. "Hi, Della." Pretty close. She asked him if she could stay with Sharee, and he explained that they'd found it better not to let relatives or significant others stay with the patient during the procedure. Sharee let go her hand with a big smile. She liked Dr. Rourke, a handsome, ruddy redhead, and had told Delaware several times that she thought he was cute. She followed the nurse eagerly through a swinging door. Dr. Rourke stayed in the hall with Delaware. "She'll be fine," he said. Delaware nodded. "Aspiration is about as big a deal as a haircut," he said in his pleasant voice. He waited for her to nod, and then said, "You know, I can do that tubal ligation. It's not a big deal, she won't know the difference."

"That's the trouble," Delaware said.

He didn't get it.

"She understands this," Delaware said.

"I can explain the ligation to her. So that she'll understand that she won't have to worry about prevention any more." He was warm, urgent with generosity.

"Can you untie it?"

"She shouldn't be having," then a pause.

"She was brain damaged during birth," Delaware said. She had said it fairly often. "It isn't genetic." Living proof, she stared at the doctor. He began to look angry, like Kevin Costner, like everybody.

"Yes, all right," he said, doctors never make mistakes. "But isn't it pretty likely that she'll forget to use the diaphragm again?"

"She didn't. She doesn't forget. This jerk she knows took her to a drive-in and came on to her in the car. So like she doesn't want some date rapist's side effects." She stared at the doctor, who looked impatient, so that she hurried her words. "Maybe like some day she'd want to have another baby. I can't choose that for her. How could I do that?"

He took a deep breath and let it out heavily.

"All right," he said. He turned away. "She'll be fine," he said again. "Piece of cake." He went through the swinging doors.

Delaware stood awhile in the hall and then thought it was stupid to wait there. She went to ask the receptionist where the bathroom was. She had begun to need to pee while they were on the bus, even before they changed to the westside bus at Sixth.

Norman waited till he was sure Squealy Mary would be gone, but when he came back she was prissing up and down in front of the Butcher Shop as if she owned the place, straight-backed, turning around at each end of the lawn like some wind-up toy. What did her husband think he was doing letting her show herself on the street like that? They were all the same, showing their wares, prissing on their stick legs. Sucking up to Young. Oh, Mr. Young says this, Mr. Young says that. He knew what Young said. Though I speak with tongues of men and angels. He knew what Young said and he knew his own business. None of their business. They ought to be home, keeping house and keeping out of the way. He started to turn back, to go around the next block hoping she would be gone when he came back to the corner. When he realized what he was doing, he stopped short. He strode down the block straight to her. "All right," he said, "I'll take over now."

"I'm on duty," she said in her high, shaking voice.

"I said I'm taking over," he said, and watched her head bobble and tremble. But she did not move. "I'm going to tell Mr. Young about your behavior," she squealed.

"I stand here," he said.

"All right, stand there," she said, and she started parading up and down again. He stood holding up his sign. Again and again she came past him, from the left, then from the right, heels clicking on the pavement, hands by her sides, shoulders held narrowed in. Shove the stick of his sign up into her, keep her back straight! He never looked at her. He stood at his post in front of the steps of the Butcher Shop and held up his sign. God was his witness.

Sitting in the very clean green stall Delaware decided to cry, to get the tears and snot out in private while her mother was busy elsewhere, but of course they wouldn't come; she just made her throat feel sore. She unbuttoned her shirt and slipped it down to look at her right shoulder, between the neck and the shoulder cap, where she could feel the hurt of the blow of the man's sign. Nothing showed except some redness that was probably because she'd kept rubbing it with the hand Sharee wasn't holding.

Back on the sofa in the waiting room she picked up the magazine to hide behind. She read some words about something, but saw with great clarity all the time the legs and feet of the woman who had shouted about praying. She was wearing tan pantyhose and navy shoes with trim little heels. Her skirt was navy and white, white dots on navy, with pleats. Above that Delaware could not see her. She could only hear the screaming, Mom, Mom. The man was wearing slacks, brown slacks and brown shoes, and a striped shirt. He had a saggy belly because he was old, but he had no face, because he was shaking the possum sign in front of it with that chopping motion, as if it was an ax, first up and down, then closer and closer to Sharee and Delaware, as they came closer and closer, till he hit.

She flinched.

"Delaware is a pretty name," Kathryn said behind the reception desk, and after a while the words came across to Delaware. "Where did you get that name?"

"My mother just liked how it sounded."

"It's unusual."

"There's Indiana Jones."

Kathryn laughed and nodded. She sorted papers in a file. "Just you and her live together?"

Delaware didn't mind, because Kathryn's voice was easy, or because her sugar-brown face looked tired now that it didn't look angry. "Yeah," she said.

"You in high school?"

"Yeah."

"Job?"

"Summers. She works at the Frost-T-Man. She always works."

"That's good," Kathryn said softly. She sorted some more and after a while said, "You doing OK in high school," not a question but as if she knew.

"Yeah."

"I bet you do. Go on to college?"

"Yeah I guess."

"That's good," Kathryn said again. "You'll do it."

The tears arrived suddenly and quietly and poured out and dried up. Delaware read reviews of a movie about a man who killed twenty women and a movie about children possessed by demons. The nurse came to the end of the hall and said, "Your friend's in recovery now, honey."

Delaware followed her down the hall. The nurse talked to her without turning around. "She was a little nervous so Doctor gave her a tranquillizer. She'll be a little woozy for half an hour, maybe. Then she can get dressed." She led Delaware into a clean, green, windowless room with three beds in it, two of them empty. Sharee was tucked into one, her curly, thick hair pulled back and her face without makeup, so that she looked like a kid. She focussed on Delaware and smiled sleepily. "Hi, baby!" she said.

THE SPOONS IN THE BASEMENT

Georgia was standing on a desk chair cleaning out the high shelves of the closet in her daughter Rose's room when her hand, groping blind on the topmost corner shelf for whatever might be there, came upon a flattish, angled object. Brought down to daylight, this proved to be a small leather-covered box with a delicate catch, opening to reveal a set of apostle spoons, silver with gilt bowls, ranged on blue velvet. Not twelve different apostles, as in the very grand sets, but six identicals, minutely bearded, charming, and doubtless valuable. Georgia's house had had a good many owners since it was built in 1899; and one of them, leaving for the holidays in June of 1910 or for a year abroad in September of 1951, in the flurry of the last day's cleaning up and packing, stuck the apostle spoons and perhaps the silver candlesticks up in that high dark corner, safe from Jean Valjean himself, and returned in a month or a year and retrieved the candlesticks but forgot the spoons, until the occasion arose to dust off the demi-tasses for company, and then it was, James, have you any idea what I did with those spoons Aunt Edith gave us? The little coffee spoons? And moved to San Diego or Saskatchewan, and let bygones be bygones, except for the small pang of auld lang syne regret when-

81

ever she got out the demi-tasses. I do wonder what ever happened to those spoons!

Georgia accepted them with gratitude, compunction, and superstition, as a gift from the house itself. It was a house of some character, though no architectural distinction: a western-style Victorian frame house with basement, two floors, full attic, and endless closets to hide spoons in. Georgia and her husband had come to it a few years earlier with one baby, and two more had been born to them while they lived in it. To these children the house was the center of the world, the original referent of the word "home," unconfused by the echoes their parents heard in the word, resonances of other centers and beginnings. On the family's first night in it, amidst the packing crates, the house had made a very loud noise at an indefinable location upstairs, and now and then its doors opened softly on business of their own, but it had never been frightening or even strange; and its disclosure now of the coffee spoons seemed to Georgia to seal a bond. It had accepted her. She gave it love and care, it gave her shelter and spoons. Perceiving it thus, she was delighted by the transaction. She and her husband bought six demi-tasses to use with the coffee spoons, and continued to use them and to inhabit the house, as the children grew up in it and left it one by one.

It was about fifteen years after finding the apostle spoons that, without knowing which room of the house she was in or which wall of the room the door was in, Georgia went through the door to her right, and found that the house had a large basement which she had not known about before. It was floored with the same kind of blackish, use-polished concrete as the basement she had known about before, but this basement was lighter, cleaner, and far more extensive, with a calm, clear air in the corridor in which she found herself, and in which she soon met a young woman.

Though her pleasure in discovering this spacious increase to her house and her anticipation of exploring it were at first quite spoilt, and continued to be cramped, by the presence of the stranger, common sense and a certain stubborn justice let Georgia escape from mere territoriality by admitting that there was, after all, a great deal of room down here which she had never used or needed, even though, having come upon it at last, she might now want it. So she felt no animosity to the young woman, whose manner was modest, candid, and easy. As they talked, Georgia felt a liking for her, which survived the revelation that two other young women, now out at work, shared the rooms to the right of the central corridor or hall.

They were not big rooms—their occupant, not at all defensive of her squatter's rights, invited Georgia to look where she pleased—and seemed neat enough, though rather cold and crowded. There was no reason why the three friends should not have the use of them, if they liked. Georgia and her husband would merely accumulate stuff in them. Better that they be lived in.

When the guest and her host (but which was which? in Latin and French the same word, indeed; and what of the angelic host?) looked into the furnace room for a moment, the coldness of this region of the house needed no further explanation. "Yes, we have a furnace, but we don't use it," the young woman had said; and she now opened the door of the furnace room, not very wide, for a glance inside: enough. Drawing back quickly, Georgia acknowledged the good sense of not making free with that sort of furnace. The huge unvarying roar it made, and the mere slit of a glimpse of its blazing bessemer-fires, put it right out of the comfort category. Better be a little on the chilly side than try hooking vents and filters and fiddly little thermostats onto an engine of that kind. It was not domestic. Its connections were deeper. No wonder the air down here was so calm and clear!

When the young tenant showed her the big, unoccupied room at the end of the hall, Georgia's spirits expanded to fit it at once. It was like a ballroom, with its long, clean floor, unencumbered. A place to dance or to work, a big, clear workroom. Gratitude to the young women for leaving this best room free emboldened Georgia to ask what she had already been told but had not, as they say, caught (she never did catch)—that is, her tenant's name. It was Ann, and Georgia was pleased with herself for having had the courage to ask it, since she liked both the name and its owner.

But, interrupting pleasure, a door at the end of the hall to the left of the big room opened, and from outside, from the garden, it must be, how odd, came a woman of middle age, of middle size, and of unmistakably mediocre quality. She and her husband, as she announced without explanation or apology, occupied that bedroom there, down the hall from the furnace room, across from the girls' rooms. Her husband was asleep in bed, and she wasn't going to have anybody disturbing him. It was their room and none of Georgia's business.

Three quiet, responsible young women in the basement is one thing; a middle-aged couple one of whom is abrasive and the other in bed is quite another. Georgia was annoyed. Annoyance grew to outrage with a glimpse, behind the woman's belligerent yet furtive figure, of a stuffy room smelling of bedclothes and jam-full of cruets and frames and fringes, things that might very well have been stolen from upstairs. "I don't think you can stay," she said to the woman, who responded with argument, demand, and threat. "I shall call our lawyer," said Georgia in a huff, "and have you sued for arrears of rent!"

That was a triumph. An incontestable triumph: in a huff in a strange basement, to come up with a killer phrase like "arrears of rent"! The disagreeable woman withdrew in defeat (into the contested room, to be sure), and Georgia turned back to Ann, back to the long, light workroom full of air and promise. The notion of stolen goods had reminded her of something, and she felt that Ann—particularly in contrast to the other woman—could be trusted.

She explained that early last summer, a day or so before leaving for a long vacation, she had put away the silver teaspoons. These were a bizarre but endearing lot of about twenty Victorian souvenir spoons collected by her maternal grandmother, the only family teaspoons to have survived such vicissitudes as the San Francisco earthquake of 1906 and the summer tenant during the Depression who absconded with the plate. The teaspoons were not only useful but now, given the exalted price of silver, appallingly valuable; and so she had hidden them, so as not to worry about them over the summer. On returning in August she discovered that in the last-minute flurry of cleaning out and packing up she had put them away only too well, and hidden them indeed. Attic footlockers, basement shelves, kitchen recesses, all the closets, had been ransacked at intervals for weeks. The spoons remained inaccessible to burglar and owner alike. "I didn't," Georgia now said, knowing it to be impossible, and yet all things may be possible, may they not, in the basement you didn't know was there, "I didn't put those spoons down here somewhere, did I?"

Young Ann shook her head. She knew the spoons were not there. If she also knew where they were, though she looked regretful, she did not say. Only later did it occur to Georgia that her silence might be taken to mean that the house had, at long last, completed its transaction.

SUNDAY IN SUMMER
IN SEATOWN

Sunday morning they are all here. They get up late and wear pajamas in the motel room yawning. Reading the Sunday paper. Sunlight in the windows. Later they all go out for brunch. There happens the great brunch launch of many striped paunches and small wide feet in thick white cheap shoes untied and mother not smiling. Brunch is eaten and eaten and eaten and then the beach.

Each to the beach alone in families and many many Korean-American Presbyterians after service playing volleyball in praise of Jesus in Korean and other Christian-Americans also come but if they ever turn and face the waves each is heathen on the beach alone and has no nation. The waves come in to every one to each alone. All the many waves come in to them. Many do not look at them. Many turn away from them. Some kiss in dunes. The big waves break and the little children scream like gulls and run and the seagulls scream, they run and scream and fly. Their small wide feet are red. Many Americans walk on large feet that point away from each other in dirty white shoes. Many Americans jog. They jog. They jog. They jog. They jog along with heavy breaths beside the waves not looking at the waves that are not interested in their health. There happens the jogging of Americans, beside the volleyballs and gulls that fly and waves that come in as many as ever always.

Sunday afternoon the waves come in and break and the children cry and fly and slowly slowly there are fewer. The waves come in, the many waves as many as ever coming in. On the small streets the engines start. Car doors open, car doors slam. Cars are going and going and gone. The sun is sinking and sinking and sunk. The dunes where they kissed are cold.

Sunday evening they are not here but there are fires far down the beach where someone else stayed to sing. A heathen dog runs back and forth from the water's edge. The sea is grey out past the waves that bring the last light in. Where are they gone, where are they? Gone. Home to the little bright box of artificial life. Bedtime, sand in the bottom of the bed. Prayers, sunburn lotion on the tops of the little wide red feet. In their dreams fly gulls. Waves rock them with long arms. Each alone. The beach where they are not is grey and the half moon is white. The half moon sets between Sunday night and Monday morning in the distant in the horizontal in the grey sea out past the waves that are not interested.

IN THE DROUGHT

For Judith and Ruth

Sarah was watering the tomato plants, letting the water flow from the hose along the runnel between the big droopy messy bushes promiscuously mingling their green and red and yellow and little pearshaped and middlesized plumshaped and big tomatoshaped tomatoes so that she couldn't tell which one grew on which of the six plants. She ate a little yellow pearshaped one. It was like tart honey in her mouth. The marvelous bitter smell of the leaves was on her hands now. She thought it was time to get a basket and pick some of the reddest and yellowest ones, but only after she finished watering; there were still the two old roses needing a drink, and the youngest azalea looked very thirsty. Late afternoon light struck through the air at a long angle, making the water from the hose seem reddish. She looked again; there must be rust coming through the pipes. The flow from the end of the hose was reddish-brown, and increasingly opaque. She held up the hose and let the stream arch out so she could watch it. The color deepened fast to crimson. Striking the earth it made puddles of that intense and somber color on the dirt, slow to soak in. She had not touched the faucet, but the flow had increased. The red stream shooting from the end of the hose looked thick, almost solid. She did not want to touch it.

She set the hose down in the runnel and went to the standpipe to turn it off. It seemed wrong to water plants with water that looked like that. Puzzled and uneasy, she went up the two back stairs and into the kitchen, hooking the screen door shut behind her with a practised foot. Belle was standing at the sink. "There's something funny," Sarah began, but Belle looked at her and said, "Look."

From the arched steel faucet ran a red stream, spattering on the white enamel of the sink and pooling in the strainer before it ran down the drain.

"It must be the hotwater heater," Belle said.

"The garden hose is doing it too," Sarah said.

After a while Belle said, "It must be the drought. Something in the reservoirs. Mud from the bottom of the lakes, or something."

"Turn it off," Sarah said.

Belle turned off the hot tap. Then slowly, as if compelled, she turned on the cold tap. The red, thick flow spurted out, spattering heavily. Belle put her finger into the stream. "Don't!" Sarah said.

"It's hot," Belle said. "Almost hot." She turned it off.

They watched the red drops and splatters slide sluggishly towards the drain.

"Should we call the plumber?" Belle said, "No, I guess not— but the city water thing, water department, bureau? Do you think? But I suppose it's happening to everybody, everybody would be calling at once, wouldn't they. Like earthquakes."

Sarah went into the front room and looked out the picture window, over the brown grass and across the street. The lawn sprinkler on the Mortensons' lawn was still going. Sunday evening was one of the two days a week watering was permitted under the drought restrictions. You were supposed to water only by hand and only shrubs and vegetable gardens, but Mr. Mortenson turned on his little lawn sprinkler and nobody said anything or reported him. He was a big man with two big teen-age sons who rode motorbikes. He never spoke to Belle and Sarah and never looked at them. The sons never spoke, but sometimes they looked, staring while they talked with their friends who came in pickups and on motorbikes. Mr. Mortenson was in his carport cutting firewood, the whine of the power saw rising to a scream, stopping abruptly, starting again. Mrs. Mortenson had gone by an hour ago on her way to church; she went morning and evening on Sundays. She always looked away from Belle and Sarah's house when she passed it.

The telephone rang, and Sarah answered it to shut it up. It was Neenie. "Sarah! The darndest thing! You won't believe! I went to pee and I looked in the toilet, you know, I just noticed, and it was all *red* and I thought, oh, my heavens, I've got my period, and then I thought, but I'm sixty-*six*! and I had a hysterectomy, didn't I? and so I thought, oh, oh no, it's my kidneys, I'm going to die, but I went to wash my hands, and the water came out of the *faucets* all red. So it isn't me, it has to be the city water, isn't that the strangest thing? Maybe some kind of fraternity joke thing? Eleanor thinks it's mud, because the water up in the watershed is so low, from the drought, but I called the city and they said nobody had reported any abnormalities. I don't suppose your water's coming funny, is it?"

"Yes," Sarah said, standing watching the low sunlight strike through the crystal showers from Mr. Mortenson's sprinkler. "Listen, Neenie, I'll call you back, I have to make a call now. Don't worry about it. OK?"

"No, no, I won't worry, it just seems so strange, goodbye," Neenie said hurriedly. "Love to Belle!"

Sarah called Andrew and got his recorded voice: "Hullo! Sorry, Tom and I aren't doing the telephone just now; but we'll get back to you soon." She waited for the beep and said, "Andrew, this is Sarah," and paused, and said, "Is there something funny with—"

and Andrew came on the line: "Hullo, Sarah! I was monitoring. Tom says I mustn't feel guilty about monitoring."

"Andrew, this is weird, but is your water OK? your tap water?"

"Should I look?"

"Yes, would you?"

While Sarah waited, Belle came into the room. She straightened the afghan on the sofa and stood looking out across the street.

"Their water looks all right," she said.

Sarah nodded.

"Rainbows," Belle said.

Andrew came back on the line after a considerable time. "Hello, Sarah. Did you taste it?"

"No," she said, seeing again the thick, strong, bright-red rush of it from the hose.

"I did," he said, and paused. "I asked Mrs. Simpson in the apartment downstairs. They have water. Not—what we have."

"What should we do?" Sarah said.

"Call the city," he said vigorously. "We pay for our water. They can't let this happen!"

"*Let* it happen?"

After a little while Andrew said, "Well, then, *we* can't let it happen."

"I'll call around," Sarah said.

"Do that. I'll call Sandy at the paper. We can't just . . ."

"No," she said. "We can't. Call me back if you find out anything. Or decide anything."

"You too. OK? Talk to you soon. Chin up, not the end of the world!" He hung up; Sarah hung up and turned to Belle. "We'll get something going," she said. "There's a good network."

Belle went back to the kitchen, and Sarah followed her. Belle turned both taps full on. The red rush from the faucet spattered and coiled on the enamel. "Don't, don't," Sarah whispered, but Belle put her hands in the stream, turning and rubbing them together, washing them. "There are songs about this," she said. "But they're not my songs." She turned off the taps and deliberately wiped her hands on the white-and-yellow dishtowel, leaving great smears and clots that would soon stiffen and turn brown. "I don't like city water," she said. "Never did. Or small town water. It tastes funny. Tastes like sweat. Up in the mountains, you could drink from little creeks that run right out of the glaciers, out of the snowmelt. Like drinking air. Drinking sky. Bubbles without the champagne. I want to go back up to the mountains, Sarah."

"We'll go," Sarah said. "We'll go soon." They held each other for a while, close, silent.

"What *are* we going to drink?" Sarah whispered. Her voice shook.

Belle loosened her hold and leaned back a bit; she stroked Sarah's hair back from her face. "Milk," she said. "We'll drink milk, love."

ETHER, OR

For the Narrative Americans

Edna

I never go in the Two Blue Moons any more. I thought about that when I was arranging the grocery window today and saw Corrie go in across the street and open up. Never did go into a bar alone in my life. Sook came by for a candy bar and I said that to her, said I wonder if I ought to go have a beer there sometime, see if it tastes different on your own. Sook said Oh Ma you always been on your own. I said I seldom had a moment to myself and four husbands, and she said You know that don't count. Sook's fresh. Breath of fresh air. I saw Needless looking at her with that kind of dog look men get. I was surprised to find it gave me a pang, I don't know what of. I just never saw Needless look that way. What did I expect, Sook is twenty and the man is human. He just always seemed like he did fine on his own. Independent. That's why he's restful. Silvia died years and years and years ago, but I never thought of it before as a long time. I wonder if I have mistaken him. All this time working for him. That would be a strange thing. That was what the pang felt like, like when you know you've made some kind of mistake, been stupid, sewn the seam inside out, left the burner on.

They're all strange, men are. I guess if I understood them I wouldn't find them so interesting. But Toby Walker, of them all he was the strangest. The stranger. I never knew where he was coming from. Roger came out of the desert, Ady came out of the ocean, but Toby came from farther. But he was here when I came. A lovely man, dark all through, dark as forests. I lost my way in him. I loved to lose my way in him. How I wish it was then, not now! Seems like I can't get lost any more. There's only one way to go. I have to keep plodding along it. I feel like I was walking across Nevada, like the pioneers, carrying a lot of stuff I need, but as I go along I have to keep dropping off things. I had a piano once but it got swamped at a crossing of the Platte. I had a good frypan but it got too heavy and I left it in the Rockies. I had a couple ovaries but they wore out around the time we were in the Carson Sink. I had a good memory but pieces of it keep dropping off, have to leave them scattered around in the sagebrush, on the sand hills. All the kids are still coming along, but I don't have them. I had them, it's not the same as having them. They aren't with me any more, even Archie and Sook. They're all walking along back where I was years ago. I wonder will they get any nearer than I have to the west side of the mountains, the valleys of the orange groves? They're years behind me. They're still in Iowa. They haven't even thought about the Sierras yet. I didn't either till I got here. Now I begin to think I'm a member of the Donner Party.

Thos. Sunn

The way you can't count on Ether is a hindrance sometimes, like when I got up in the dark this morning to catch the minus tide and stepped out the door in my rubber boots and plaid jacket with my clam spade and bucket, and overnight she'd gone inland again. The damn desert and the damn sagebrush. All you could dig up there with your damn spade would be a God damn fossil. Personally I blame it on the Indians. I do not believe that a fully civilised country would allow these kind of irregularities in a town. However as I have lived here since 1949 and could not sell my house and property for chicken feed, I intend to finish up here, like it or not. That should take a few more years, ten or fifteen most likely. Although you can't count on anything these days anywhere let alone a place like this. But I like to look after myself, and I can do it here. There is not so much Government meddling and interference and general hindering in Ether as you would find in the cities. This may be because it isn't usually where the Government thinks it is, though it is, sometimes.

When I first came here I used to take some interest in a woman, but it is my belief that in the long run a man does better not to. A woman is a worse hindrance to a man than anything else, even the Government.

I have read the term "a crusty old bachelor" and would be willing to say that that describes me so long as the crust goes all the way through. I don't like things soft in the center. Softness is no use in this hard world. I am like one of my mother's biscuits.

My mother, Mrs. J. J. Sunn, died in Wichita, KS, in 1944, at the age of 79. She was a fine woman and my experience of women in general does not apply to her in particular.

Since they invented the kind of biscuits that come in a tube which you hit on the edge of the counter and the dough explodes out of it under pressure, that's the kind I buy, and by baking them about one half hour they come out pretty much the way I like them, crust clear through. I used to bake the dough all of a piece, but then discovered that you can break it apart into separate biscuits. I don't hold with reading directions and they are always printed in small, fine print on the damn foil which gets torn when you break open the tube. I use my mother's glasses. They are a good make.

The woman I came here after in 1949 is still here. That was during my brief period of infatuation. Fortunately I can say that she did not get her hooks onto me in the end. Some other men have not been as lucky. She has married or as good as several times and was pregnant and pushing a baby carriage for decades. Sometimes I think everybody under forty in this town is one of Edna's. I had a very narrow escape. I have had a dream about Edna several times. In this dream I am out on the sea fishing for salmon from a small boat, and Edna swims up from the sea waves and tries to climb into the boat. To prevent this I hit her hands with the gutting knife and cut off the fingers, which fall into the water and turn into some kind of little creatures that swim away. I never can tell if they are babies or seals. Then Edna swims after them making a strange noise, and I see that in actuality she is a kind of seal or sea lion, like the big ones in the cave on the south coast, light brown and very large and fat and sleek in the water.

This dream disturbs me, as it is unfair. I am not the kind of man who would do such a thing. It causes me discomfort to remember the strange noise she makes in the dream, when I am in the grocery store and Edna is at the cash register. To make sure she rings it up right and I get the right change, I have to look at her hands opening and shutting the drawers and her fingers working on the keys. What's wrong with women is that you can't count on them. They are not fully civilised.

Roger Hiddenstone

I only come into town sometimes. It's a now and then thing. If the road takes me there, fine, but I don't go hunting for it. I run a two hundred thousand acre cattle ranch, which gives me a good deal to do. I'll look up sometimes and the moon is new that I saw full last night. One summer comes after another like steers through a chute. In the winters, though, sometimes the weeks freeze like the creek water, and things hold still for a while. The air can get still and clear in the winter here in the high desert. I have seen the mountain peaks from Baker and Rainier in the north, Hood and Jefferson, Three-Fingered Jack and the Sisters east of here, on south to Shasta and Lassen, all standing up in the sunlight for eight hundred or a thousand miles. That was when I was flying. From the ground you can't see that much of the ground, though you can see the rest of the universe, nights.

I traded in my two-seater Cessna for a quarterhorse mare, and I generally keep a Ford pickup, though at times I've had a Chevrolet. Any one of them will get me in to town so long as there isn't more than a couple feet of snow on the road. I like to come in now and then and have a Denver omelette at the café for breakfast, and a visit with my wife and son. I have a drink at the Two Blue Moons, and spend the night at the motel. By the next morning I'm ready to go back to the ranch to find out what went wrong while I was gone. It's always something.

Edna was only out to the ranch once while we were married. She spent three weeks. We were so busy in the bed I don't recall much else about it, except the time she tried to learn to ride. I put her on Sally, the cutting horse I traded the Cessna plus fifteen hundred dollars for, a highly reliable horse and more intelligent than most Republicans. But Edna had that mare morally corrupted within ten minutes. I was trying to explain how she'd interpret what you did with your knees, when Edna started yipping and raking her like a bronc rider. They lit out of the yard and went halfway to Ontario at a dead run. I was riding the old roan gelding and only met them coming back. Sally was unrepentant, but Edna was sore and delicate that evening. She claimed all the love had been jolted out of her. I guess that this was true, in the larger sense, since it wasn't long after that that she asked to go back to Ether. I thought she had quit her job at the grocery, but she had only asked for a month off, and she said Needless would want her for the extra business at Christmas. We drove back to town, finding it a little west of where we had left it, in a very pretty location near the Ochoco Mountains, and we had a happy Christmas season in Edna's house with the children.

I don't know whether Archie was begotten there or at the ranch. I'd like to think it was at the ranch so that there would be that in him drawing him to come back some day. I don't know who to leave all this to. Charlie Echeverria is good with the stock, but can't think ahead two days and couldn't deal with the buyers, let alone the corporations. I don't want the corporations profiting from this place. The hands are nice young fellows, but they don't stay put, or want to. Cowboys don't want land. Land owns you. You have to give in to that. I feel sometimes like all the stones on two hundred thousand acres were weighing on me, and my mind's gone to rimrock. And the beasts wandering and calling across all that land. The cows stand with their young calves in the wind that blows March snow like frozen sand across the flats. Their patience is a thing I try to understand.

Gracie Fane

I saw that old rancher on Main Street yesterday, Mr. Hiddenstone, was married to Edna once. He acted like he knew where he was going, but when the street ran out onto the sea cliff he sure did look foolish. Turned round and came back in those high-heel boots, long legs, putting his feet down like a cat the way cowboys do. He's a skinny old man. He went into the Two Blue Moons. Going to try to drink his way back to eastern Oregon, I guess. I don't care if this town is east or west. I don't care if it's anywhere. It never is anywhere anyway. I'm going to leave here and go to Portland, to the Intermountain, the big trucking company, and be a truck driver. I learned to drive when I was five on my grandpa's tractor. When I was ten I started driving my dad's Dodge Ram, and I've driven pickups and delivery vans for Mom and Mr. Needless ever since I got my license. Jase gave me lessons on his eighteen-wheeler last summer. I did real good. I'm a natural. Jase said so. I never got to get out onto the I-5 but only once or twice, though. He kept saying I needed more practice pulling over and parking and shifting up and down. I didn't mind practicing, but then when I got her stopped he'd want to get me into this bed thing he fixed up behind the seats and pull my jeans off, and we had to screw some before he'd go on teaching me anything. My own idea would be to drive a long way and learn a lot and then have some sex and coffee and then drive back a different way, maybe on hills where I'd have to practice braking and stuff. But I guess men have different priorities. Even when I was driving he'd have his arm around my back and be petting my boobs. He has these huge hands can reach right across both boobs at once. It felt good, but it interfered with his concentration teaching me. He would say *Oh baby you're so great* and I would think he meant I was driving great but then he'd start making those sort of groaning noises and I'd have to shift down and find a place to pull out and get in the bed thing again. I used to practice changing gears in my mind when we were screwing and it helped. I could shift him right up and down again. I used to yell *Going eighty!* when I got him really shifted up. *Fuzz on your tail!* And make these sireen noises. That's my CB name: Sireen. Jase got his route shifted in August. I made my plans then. I'm driving for the grocery and saving money till I'm seventeen and go to Portland to work for the Intermountain Company. I want to drive the I-5 from Seattle to LA, or get a run to Salt Lake City. Till I can buy my own truck. I got it planned out.

Tobinye Walker

The young people all want to get out of Ether. Young Americans in a small town want to get up and go. And some do, and some come to a time when they stop talking about where they're going to go when they go. They have come to where they are. Their problem, if it's a problem, isn't all that different from mine. We have a window of opportunity; it closes. I used to walk across the years as easy as a child here crosses the street, but I went lame, and had to stop walking. So this is my time, my heyday, my floruit.

When I first knew Edna she said a strange thing to me; we had been talking, I don't remember what about, and she stopped and gazed at me. "You have a look on you like an unborn child," she said. "You look at things like an unborn child." I don't know what I answered, and only later did I wonder how she knew how an unborn child looks, and whether she meant a fetus in the womb or a child that never came to be conceived. Maybe she meant a newborn child. But I think she used the word she meant to use.

When I first stopped by here, before my accident, there was no town, of course, no settlement. Several peoples came through and sometimes encamped for a season, but it was a range without boundary, though it had names. At that time people didn't have the expectation of stability they have now; they knew that so long as a river keeps running it's a river. Nobody but the beavers built dams, then. Ether always covered a lot of territory, and it has retained that property. But its property is not continuous.

The people I used to meet coming through generally said they came down Humbug Creek from the river in the mountains, but Ether itself never has been in the Cascades, to my knowledge. Fairly often you can see them to the west of it, though usually it's west of them, and often west of the Coast Range in the timber or the dairy country, sometimes right on the sea. It has a broken range. It's an unusual place. I'd like to go back to the center to tell about it, but I can't walk any more. I have to do my flourishing here.

J. Needless

People think there are no Californians. Nobody can come from the promise land. You have to be going to it. Die in the desert, grave by the wayside. I come from California, born there, think about it some. I was born in the Valley of San Arcadio. Orchards. Like a white bay of orange flowers under bare blue-brown mountains. Sunlight like air, like clear water, something you lived in, an element. Our place was a little farmhouse up in the foothills, looking out over the valley. My father was a manager for one of the companies. Oranges flower white, with a sweet, fine scent. Outskirts of Heaven, my mother said once, one morning when she was hanging out the wash. I remember her saying that. We live on the outskirts of Heaven.

She died when I was six and I don't remember a lot but that about her. Now I have come to realise that my wife has been dead so long that I have lost her too. She died when our daughter Corrie was six. Seemed like there was some meaning in it at the time, but if there was I didn't find it.

Ten years ago when Corrie was twenty-one she said she wanted to go to Disneyland for her birthday. With me. Damn if she didn't drag me down there. Spent a good deal to see people dressed up like mice with water on the brain and places made to look like places they weren't. I guess that is the point there. They clean dirt till it is a sanitary substance and spread it out to look like dirt so you don't have to touch dirt. You and Walt are in control there. You can be in any kind of place, space or the ocean or castles in Spain, all sanitary, no dirt. I would have liked it as a boy, when I thought the idea was to run things. Changed my ideas, settled for a grocery.

Corrie wanted to see where I grew up, so we drove over to San Arcadio. It wasn't there, not what I meant by it. Nothing but roofs, houses, streets and houses. Smog so thick it hid the mountains and the sun looked green. God damn, get me out of there, I said, they have changed the color of the sun. Corrie wanted to look for the house but I was serious. Get me out of here, I said, this is the right place but the wrong year. Walt Disney can get rid of the dirt on his property if he likes, but this is going too far. This is my property.

I felt like that. Like I thought it was something I had, but they scraped all the dirt off and underneath was cement and some electronic wiring. I'd as soon not have seen that. People come through here say how can you stand living in a town that doesn't stay in the same place all the time, but have they been to Los Angeles? It's anywhere you want to say it is.

Well, since I don't have California what have I got? A good enough business. Corrie's still here. Good head on her. Talks a lot. Runs that bar like a bar should be run. Runs her husband pretty well too. What do I mean when I say I had a mother, I had a wife? I mean remembering what orange flowers smell like, whiteness, sunlight. I carry that with me. Corinna and Silvia, I carry their names. But what do I have?

What I don't have is right within hand's reach every day. Every day but Sunday. But I can't reach out my hand. Every man in town gave her a child and all I ever gave her was her week's wages. I know she trusts me. That's the trouble. Too late now. Hell, what would she want me in her bed for, the Medicare benefits?

Emma Bodely

Everything is serial killers now. They say everyone is naturally fascinated by a man planning and committing one murder after another without the least reason and not even knowing who he kills personally. There was the man up in the city recently who tortured and tormented three tiny little boys and took photographs of them while he tortured them and of their corpses after he killed them. Authorities are talking now about what they ought to do with these photographs. They could make a lot of money from a book of them. He was apprehended by the police as he lured yet another tiny boy to come with him, as in a nightmare. There were men in California and Texas and I believe Chicago who dismembered and buried innumerably. Then of course it goes back in history to Jack the Ripper who killed poor women and was supposed to be a member of the Royal Family of England, and no doubt before his time there were many other serial killers, many of them members of Royal Families or Emperors and Generals who killed thousands and thousands of people. But in wars they kill people more or less simultaneously, not one by one, so that they are mass murderers, not serial killers, but I'm not sure

I see the difference, really. Since for the person being murdered it only happens once.

I should be surprised if we had a serial killer in Ether. Most of the men were soldiers in one of the wars, but they would be mass murderers, unless they had desk jobs. I can't think who here would be a serial killer. No doubt I would be the last to find out. I find being invisible works both ways. Often I don't see as much as I used to when I was visible. Being invisible however I'm less likely to become a serial victim.

It's odd how the natural fascination they talk about doesn't include the serial victims. I suppose it is because I taught young children for thirty-five years, but perhaps I am unnatural, because I think about those three little boys. They were three or four years old. How strange that their whole life was only a few years, like a cat. In their world suddenly instead of their mother there was a man who told them how he was going to hurt them and then did it, so that there was nothing in their life at all but fear and pain. So they died in fear and pain. But all the reporters tell is the nature of the mutilations and how decomposed they were, and that's all about them. They were little boys not men. They are not fascinating. They are just dead. But the serial killer they tell all about over and over and discuss his psychology and how his parents caused him to be so fascinating, and he lives forever, as witness Jack the Ripper and Hitler the Ripper. Everyone around here certainly remembers the name of the man who serially raped and photographed the tortured little boys before he serially murdered them. He was named Westley Dodd but what were their names?

Of course we the people murdered him back. That was what he wanted. He wanted us to murder him. I cannot decide if hanging him was a mass murder or a serial murder. We all did it, like a war, so it is a mass murder, but we each did it, democratically, so I suppose it is serial, too. I would as soon be a serial victim as a serial murderer, but I was not given the choice.

My choices have become less. I never had a great many, as my sexual impulses were not appropriate to my position in life, and no one I fell in love with knew it. I am glad when Ether turns up in a different place as it is kind of like a new choice of where to live, only I didn't have to make it. I am capable only of very small choices. What to eat for breakfast, oatmeal or corn flakes, or perhaps only a piece of fruit? Kiwi fruits were fifteen cents apiece at the grocery and I bought half a dozen. A while ago they were the most exotic thing, from New Zealand I think and a dollar each, and now they raise them all over the Willamette Valley. But then, the Willamette Valley may be quite exotic to a person in New Zealand. I like the way they're cool in your mouth, the same way the flesh of them looks cool, a smooth green you can see into, like jade stone. I still see things like that perfectly clearly. It's only with people that my eyes are more and more transparent, so that I don't always see what they're doing, and so that they can look right through me as if my eyes were air and say, "Hi, Emma, how's life treating you?"

Life's treating me like a serial victim, thank you.

I wonder if she sees me or sees through me. I don't dare look. She is shy and lost in her crystal dreams. If only I could look after her. She needs looking after. A cup of tea. Herbal tea, echinacea maybe, I think her immune system needs strengthening. She is not a practical person. I am a very practical person. Far below her dreams.

Lo still sees me. Of course Lo is a serial killer as far as birds are concerned, and moles, but although it upsets me when the bird's not dead yet it's not the same as the man taking photographs. Mr. Hiddenstone once told me that cats have the instinct to let a mouse or bird stay alive awhile in order to take it to the kittens and train them to hunt, so what seems to be cruelty is thoughtfulness. Now I know that some tom cats kill kittens, and I don't think any tom ever raised kittens and trained them thoughtfully to hunt. The queen cat does that. A tom cat is the Jack the Ripper of the Royal Family. But Lo is neutered, so he might behave like a queen or at least like a kind of uncle if there were kittens around, and bring them his birds to hunt. I don't know. He doesn't mix with other cats much. He stays pretty close to home, keeping an eye on the birds and moles and me. I know that my invisibility is not universal when I wake up in the middle of the night and Lo is sitting on the bed right beside my pillow purring and looking very intently at me. It's a strange thing to do, a little uncanny. His eyes wake me, I think. But it's a good waking, knowing that he can see me, even in the dark.

Edna

All right now, I want an answer. All my life since I was fourteen I have been making my soul. I don't know what else to call it, that's what I called it then, when I was fourteen and came into the possession of my life and the knowledge of my responsibility. Since then I have not had time to find a better name for it. The word responsible means that you have to answer. You can't not answer. You'd might rather not answer, but you have to. When you answer you are making your soul, so that it has a shape to it, and size, and some staying power. I understood that, I came into that knowledge, when I was thirteen and early fourteen, that long winter in the Siskiyous. All right, so ever since then, more or less, I have worked according to that understanding. And I have worked. I have done what came into my hands to do, and I've done it the best I could and with all the mind and strength I had to give to it. There have been jobs, waitressing and clerking, but first of all and always the ordinary work of raising the children and keeping the house so that people can live decently and in health and some degree of peace of mind. Then there is responding to the needs of men. That seems like it should come first. People might say I never thought of anything but answering what men asked, pleasing men and pleasing myself, and goodness knows such questions are a joy to answer if asked by a pleasant man. But in the order of my mind, the children come before the fathers of the children.

Maybe I see it that way because I was the eldest daughter and there were four younger than me and my father had gone off. Well, all right then, those are my responsibilities as I see them, those are the questions I have tried always to answer: can people live in this house, and how does a child grow up rightly, and how to be trustworthy.

But now I have my own question. I never asked questions, I was so busy answering them, but am sixty years old this winter and think I should have time for a question. But it's hard to ask. Here it is. It's like all the time I was working keeping house and raising the kids and making love and earning our keep I thought there was going to come a time or there would be some place where all of it all came together. Like it was words I was saying, all my life, all the kinds of work, just a word here and a word there, but finally all the words would make a sentence, and I could read the sentence. I would have made my soul and know what it was for.

But I have made my soul and I don't know what to do with it. Who wants it? I have lived sixty years. All I'll do from now on is the same as what I have done only less of it, while I get weaker and sicker and smaller all the time, shrinking and shrinking around myself, and die. No matter what I did, or made, or know. The words don't mean anything. I ought to talk with Emma about this. She's the only one who doesn't say stuff like, "You're only as old as you think you are," "Oh Edna you'll never be old," rubbish like that. Toby Walker wouldn't talk that way either, but he doesn't say much at all any more. Keeps his sentence to himself. My kids that still live here, Archie and Sook, they don't want to hear anything about it. Nobody young can afford to believe in getting old.

So is all the responsibility you take only useful then, but no use later—disposable? What's the use, then? All the work you did is just gone. It doesn't make anything. But I may be wrong. I hope so, I would like to have more trust in dying. Maybe it's worth while, like some kind of answering, coming into another place.

Like I felt that winter in the Siskiyous, walking on the snow road between black firs under all the stars, that I was the same size as the universe, the same *thing* as the universe. And if I kept on walking ahead there was this glory waiting for me. In time I would come into glory. I knew that. So that's what I made my soul for. I made it for glory.

And I have known a good deal of glory. I'm not ungrateful. But it doesn't last. It doesn't come together to make a place where you can live, a house. It's gone and the years go. What's left? Shrinking and forgetting and thinking about aches and acid indigestion and cancers and pulse rates and bunions until the whole world is a room that smells like urine, is that what all the work comes to, is that the end of the babies' kicking legs, the children's eyes, the loving hands, the wild rides, the light on water, the stars over the snow? Somewhere inside it all there has to still be the glory.

Ervin Muth

I have been watching Mr. "Toby" Walker for a good while, checking up on things, and if I happened to be called upon to I could state with fair certainty that this "Mr. Walker" is *not an American*. My research has taken me considerably farther afield than that. But there are these "gray areas" or some things which many people as a rule are unprepared to accept. It takes training.

My attention was drawn to these kind of matters in the first place by scrutinizing the town records on an entirely different subject of research. Suffice it to say that I was checking the title on the Fane place at the point in time when Mrs. Osey Jean Fane put the property into the hands of Ervin Muth Relaty, of which I am proprietor. There had been a dispute concerning the property line on the east side of the Fane property in 1939 into which, due to being meticulous concerning these kind of detailed responsibilities, I checked. To my surprise I was amazed to discover that the adjoining lot, which had been developed in 1906, had been in the name of Tobinye Walker since that date, 1906! I naturally assumed at that point in time that this "Tobinye Walker" was "Mr. Toby Walker's" father and thought little more about the issue until my researches into another matter, concerning the Essel/Emmer lots, in the town records indicated that the name "Tobinye Walker" was shown as purchaser of a livery stable on that site (on Main St. between Rash St. and Goreman Ave.) in 1880.

While purchasing certain necessaries in the Needless Grocery Store soon after, I encountered Mr. Walker in person. I remarked in a jocular vein that I had been meeting his father and grandfather. This was of course a mere pleasantry. Mr. "Toby" Walker responded in what struck me as a suspicious fashion. There was some taking aback going on. Although with laughter. His exact words, to which I can attest, were the following: "I had no idea that you were capable of travelling in time!"

This was followed by my best efforts to seriously inquire concerning the persons of his same name which my researches in connection with my work as a relator had turned up. These were only met with facetious remarks such as, "I've lived here quite a while, you see," and, "Oh, I remember when Lewis and Clark came through," a statement in reference to the celebrated explorers of the Oregon Trail, who I ascertained later to have been in Oregon in 1806.

Soon after, Mr. Toby Walker "*walked*" away, thus ending the conversation.

I am convinced by evidence that "Mr. Walker" is an illegal immigrant from a foreign country who has assumed the name of a Founding Father of this fine community, that is to wit the Tobinye Walker who purchased the livery stable in 1880. I have my reasons.

My research shows conclusively that the Lewis and Clark Expedition sent by President Thos. Jefferson did not pass through any of the localities which our fine community of Ether has occupied over the course of its history. Ether never got that far north.

If Ether is to progress to fulfill its destiny as a Destination Resort on the beautiful Oregon Coast and Desert as I visualize it with a complete downtown entertainment center and entrepreneurial business community, including hub motels, RV facilities, and a Theme Park, the kind of thing that is represented by "Mr." Walker will have to go. It is the American way to buy and sell houses and properties continually in the course of moving for the sake of upward mobility and self-improvement. Stagnation is the enemy of the American way. The same person owning the same property since 1906 is unnatural and Unamerican. Ether is an American town and moves all the time. That is its destiny. I can call myself an expert.

Starra Walinow Amethyst

I keep practicing love. I was in love with that French actor Gerard but it's really hard to say his last name. Frenchmen attract me. When I watch *Star Trek The Next Generation* reruns I'm in love with Captain Jean-Luc Picard, but I can't stand Commander Riker. I used to be in love with Heathcliff when I was twelve and Miss Freff gave me *Wuthering Heights* to read. And I was in love with Sting for a while before he got weirder. Sometimes I think I am in love with Lieutenant Worf but that is pretty weird, with all those sort of wrinkles and horns on his forehead, since he's a Klingon, but that's not really what's weird. I mean it's just in the TV that he's an alien. Really he is a human named Michael Dorn. That is so weird to me. I mean I never have seen a real black person except in movies and TV. Everybody in Ether is white. So a black person would actually be an alien here. I thought what it would be like if somebody like that came into like the drug store, really tall, with that dark brown skin and dark eyes and those very soft lips that look like they could get hurt so easily, and asked for something in that really, really deep voice. Like, "Where would I find the aspirin?" And I would show him where the aspirin kind of stuff is. He would be standing beside me in front of the shelf, really big and tall and dark, and I'd feel warmth coming out of him like out of an iron woodstove. He'd say to me in a very low voice, "I don't belong in this town," and I'd say back, "I don't either," and he'd say, "Do you want to come with me?" only really really nicely, not like a come-on but like two prisoners whispering how to get out of prison together. I'd nod, and he'd say, "Back of the gas station, at dusk."

At dusk.

I love that word. Dusk. It sounds like his voice.

Sometimes I feel weird thinking about him like this. I mean because he is actually real. If it was just Worf, that's OK, because Worf is just this alien in some old reruns of a show. But there is actually Michael Dorn. So thinking about him in a sort of story that way makes me uncomfortable sometimes, because it's like I was making him a toy, something I can do anything with, like a doll. That seems like it was unfair to him. And it makes me sort of embarrassed when I think about how he actually has his own life with nothing to do with this dumb girl in some hick town he never heard of. So I try to make up somebody else to make that kind of stories about. But it doesn't work.

I really tried this spring to be in love with Morrie Stromberg, but it didn't work. He's really beautiful-looking. It was when I saw him shooting baskets that I thought maybe I could be in love with him. His legs and arms are long and smooth and he moves smooth and looks kind of like a mountain lion, with a low forehead and short dark blond hair, tawny colored. But all he ever does is hang out with Joe's crowd and talk about sport scores and cars, and once in class he was talking with Joe about me so I could hear, like, "Oh yeah Starra, wow, *she* reads *books*," not really mean, but kind of like I was like an alien from another planet, just totally absolutely strange. Like Worf or Michael Dorn would feel here. Like he meant OK, it's OK to be like that only not here. Somewhere else, OK? As if Ether wasn't already somewhere else. I mean, didn't it use to be the Indians that lived here, and now there aren't any of them either? So who belongs here and where does it belong?

About a month ago Mom told me the reason she left my father. I don't remember anything like that. I don't remember any father. I don't remember anything before Ether. She says we were living in Seattle and they had a store where they sold crystals and oils and New Age stuff, and when she got up one night to go to the bathroom he was in my room holding me. She wanted to tell me everything about how he was holding me and stuff, but I just went, "So, like, he was molesting me." And she went, "Yeah," and I said, "So what did you do?" I thought they would have had a big fight. But she said she didn't say anything, because she was afraid of him. She said, "See, to him it was like he owned me and you. And when I didn't go along with that, he would get real crazy." I think they were into a lot of pot and heavy stuff, she talks about that sometimes. So anyway next day when he went to the store she just took some of the crystals and stuff they kept at home, we still have them, and got some money they kept in a can in the kitchen just like she does here, and got on the bus to Portland with me. Somebody she met there gave us a ride here. I don't remember any of that. It's like I was born here. I asked did he ever try to look for her, and she said she didn't know but if he did he'd have a hard time finding her here. She changed her last name to Amethyst, which is her favorite stone. Walinow was her real name. She says it's Polish.

I don't know what his name was. I don't know what he did. I don't care. It's like nothing happened. I'm never going to belong to anybody.

What I know is this, I am going to love people. They will never know it. But I am going to be a great lover. I know how. I have practiced. It isn't when you belong to somebody or they belong to you or stuff. That's like Chelsey getting married to Tim because she wanted to have the wedding and the husband and a no-wax kitchen floor. She wanted stuff to belong to.

I don't want stuff, but I want practice. Like we live in this shack with no kitchen let alone a no-wax floor, and we cook on a trashburner, with a lot of crystals around, and cat pee from the strays Mom takes in, and Mom does stuff like sweeping out for Myrella's beauty parlor, and gets zits because she eats Hostess Twinkies instead of food. Mom needs to get it together. But I need to give it away.

I thought maybe the way to practice love was to have sex so I had sex with Danny last summer. Mom bought us condoms and made me hold hands with her around a bayberry candle and talk about the Passage Into Womanhood. She wanted Danny to be there too but I talked her out of it. The sex was OK but what I was really trying to do was be in love. It didn't work. Maybe it was the wrong way. He just got used to getting sex and so he kept coming around all fall, going "Hey Starra baby you know you need it." He wouldn't even say that it was him that needed it. If I need it, I can do it a lot better myself than he can. I didn't tell him that. Although I nearly did when he kept not letting me alone after I told him to stop. If he hadn't finally started going with Dana I might would have told him.

I don't know anybody else here I can be in love with. I wish I could practice on Archie but what's the use while there's Gracie Fane? It would just be dumb. I thought about asking Archie's father Mr. Hiddenstone if I could work on his ranch, next time we get near it. I could still come see Mom, and maybe there would be like ranch hands or cowboys. Or Archie would come out sometimes and there wouldn't be Gracie. Or actually there's Mr. Hiddenstone. He looks like Archie. Actually handsomer. But I guess is too old. He has a face like the desert. I noticed his eyes are the same color as Mom's turquoise ring. But I don't know if he needs a cook or anything and I suppose fifteen is too young.

J. Needless

Never have figured out where the Hohovars come from. Somebody said White Russia. That figures. They're all big and tall and heavy with hair so blond it's white and those little blue eyes. They don't look at you. Noses like new potatoes. Women don't talk. Kids don't talk. Men talk like, "Vun case yeast peggets, tree case piggle beet." Never say hello, never say goodbye, never say thanks. But honest. Pay right up in cash. When they come in town they're all dressed head to foot, the women in these long dresses with a lot of fancy stuff around the bottom and sleeves, the little girls just the same as the women, even the babies in the same long stiff skirts, all of them with bonnet things that hide their hair. Even the babies don't look up. Men and boys in long pants and shirt and coat even when it's desert here and a hundred and five in July. Something like those ammish folk on the east coast, I guess. Only the Hohovars have buttons. A lot of buttons. The vest things the women wear have about a thousand buttons. Men's flies the same. Must slow 'em down getting to the action. But everybody says buttons are no problem when they get back to their community. Everything off. Strip naked to go to their church. Tom Sunn swears to it, and Corrie says she used to sneak out there more than once on Sunday with a bunch of other kids to see the Hohovars all going over the hill buck naked, singing in their language. That would be some sight, all those tall, heavy-fleshed, white-skinned, big-ass, big-tit women parading over the hill. Barefoot, too. What the hell they do in church I don't know. Tom says they commit fornication but Tom Sunn don't know shit from a hole in the ground. All talk. Nobody I know has ever been over that hill.

Some Sundays you can hear them singing.

Now religion is a curious thing in America. According to the Christians there is only one of anything. On the contrary there seems to me to be one or more of everything. Even here in Ether we have, that I know of, Baptists of course, Methodists, Church of Christ, Lutheran, Presbyterian, Catholic though no church in town, a Quaker, a lapsed Jew, a witch, the Hohovars, and the gurus or whatever that lot in the grange are. This is not counting most people, who have no religious affiliation except on impulse.

That is a considerable variety for a town this size. What's more, they try out each other's churches, switch around. Maybe the nature of the town makes us restless. Anyhow people in Ether generally live a long time, though not as long as Toby Walker. We have time to try out different things. My daughter Corrie has been a Baptist as a teen-ager, a Methodist while in love with Jim Fry, then had a go at the Lutherans. She was married Methodist but is now the Quaker, having read a book. This may change, as lately she has been talking to the witch, Pearl W. Amethyst, and reading another book, called *Crystals and You.*

Edna says the book is all tosh. But Edna has a harder mind than most.

Edna is my religion, I guess. I was converted years ago.

As for the people in the grange, the guru people, they caused some stir when they arrived ten years ago, or is it twenty now. Maybe it was in the sixties. Seems like they've been there a long time when I think about it. My wife was still alive. Anyhow, that's a case of religion mixed up some way with politics, not that it isn't always.

When they came to Ether they had a hell of a lot of money to throw around, though they didn't throw much my way. Bought the old grange and thirty acres of pasture adjacent. Put a fence right round and God damn if they didn't electrify that fence. I don't mean the little jolt you might run in for steers but a kick would kill an elephant. Remodeled the old grange and built on barns and barracks and even a generator. Everybody inside the fence was to share everything in common with everybody else inside the fence. Though from outside the fence it looked like the guru shared a lot more of it than the rest of 'em. That was the political part. Socialism. The bubonic socialism. Rats carry it and there is no vaccine. I tell you people here were upset. Thought the whole population behind the iron curtain plus all the hippies in California were moving in next Tuesday. Talked about bringing in the National Guard to defend the rights of citizens. Personally I'd of preferred the hippies over the National Guard. Hippies were unarmed. They killed by smell alone, as people said. But at the time there was a siege mentality here. A siege inside the grange, with their electric fence and their socialism, and a siege outside the grange, with their rights of citizens to be white and not foreign and not share anything with anybody.

At first the guru people would come into the town in their orange color T-shirts, doing a little shopping, talking politely. Young people got invited into the grange. They were calling it the osh rom by then. Corrie told me about the altar with the marigolds and the big photograph of Guru Jaya Jaya Jaya. But they weren't really friendly people and they didn't get friendly treatment. Pretty soon they never came into town, just drove in and out the road gate in their orange Buicks. Sometime along in there the Guru Jaya Jaya Jaya was supposed to come from India to visit the osh rom. Never did. Went to South America instead and founded an osh rom for old Nazis, they say. Old Nazis probably have more money to share with him than young Oregonians do. Or maybe he came to find his osh rom and it wasn't where they told him.

It has been kind of depressing to see the T-shirts fade and the Buicks break down. I don't guess there's more than two Buicks and ten, fifteen people left in the osh rom. They still grow garden truck, eggplants, all kinds of peppers, greens, squash, tomatoes, corn, beans, blue and rasp and straw and marion berries, melons. Good quality stuff. Raising crops takes some skill here where the climate will change overnight. They do beautiful irrigation and don't use poisons. Seen them out there picking bugs off the plants by hand. Made a deal with them some years ago to supply my produce counter and have not regretted it. Seems like Ether is meant to be a self-sufficient place. Every time I'd get a routine set up with a supplier in Cottage Grove or Prineville, we'd switch. Have to call up and say sorry, we're on the other side of the mountains again this week, cancel those cantaloupes. Dealing with the guru people is easier. They switch along with us.

What they believe in aside from organic gardening I don't know. Seems like the Guru Jaya Jaya Jaya would take some strenuous believing, but people can put their faith in anything, I guess. Hell, I believe in Edna.

Archie Hiddenstone

Dad got stranded in town again last week. He hung around awhile to see if the range would move back east, finally drove his old Ford over to Eugene and up the McKenzie River highway to get back to the ranch. Said he'd like to stay but Charlie Echeverria would be getting into some kind of trouble if he did. He just doesn't like to stay away from the place more than a night or two. It's hard on him when we turn up way over here on the coast like this.

I know he wishes I'd go back with him. I guess I ought to. I ought to live with him. I could see Mama every time Ether was over there. It isn't that. I ought to get it straight in my mind what I want to do. I ought to go to college. I ought to get out of this town. I ought to get away.

I don't think Gracie ever actually has seen me. I don't do anything she can see. I don't drive a semi.

I ought to learn. If I drove a truck she'd see me. I could come through Ether off the I-5 or down from 84, wherever. Like that shit kept coming here last summer she was so crazy about. Used to come into the Seven-Eleven all the time for Gatorade. Called me Boy. Hey boy gimme the change in quarters. She'd be sitting up in his eighteen-wheeler playing with the gears. She never came in. Never even looked. I used to think maybe she was sitting there with her jeans off. Bareass on that truck seat. I don't know why I thought that. Maybe she was.

I don't want to drive a God damn stinking semi or try to feed a bunch of steers in a God damn desert either or sell God damn Hostess Twinkies to crazy women with purple hair either. I ought to go to college. Learn something. Drive a sports car. A Miata. Am I going to sell Gatorade to shits all my life? I ought to be somewhere that is somewhere.

I dreamed the moon was paper and I lit a match and set fire to it. It flared up just like a newspaper and started dropping down fire on the roofs, scraps of burning. Mama came out of the grocery and said, "That'll take the ocean." Then I woke up. I heard the ocean where the sagebrush hills had been.

I wish I could make Dad proud of me anywhere but the ranch. But that's the only place he lives. He won't ever ask me to come live there. He knows I can't. I ought to.

Edna

Oh how my children tug at my soul just as they tugged at my breasts, so that I want to yell Stop! I'm dry! You drank me dry years ago! Poor sweet stupid Archie. What on earth to do for him. His father found the desert he needed. All Archie's found is a tiny little oasis he's scared to leave.

I dreamed the moon was paper, and Archie came out of the house with a box of matches and tried to set it afire, and I was frightened and ran into the sea.

Ady came out of the sea. There were no tracks on that beach that morning except his, coming up towards me from the breaker line. I keep thinking about the men lately. I keep thinking about Needless. I don't know why. I guess because I never married him. Some of them I wonder why I did, how it came about. There's no reason in it. Who'd ever have thought I'd ever sleep with Tom Sunn? But how could I go on saying no to a need like that? His fly bust every time he saw me across the street. Sleeping with him was like sleeping in a cave. Dark, uncomfortable, echoes, bears farther back in. Bones. But a fire burning. Tom's true soul is that fire burning, but he'll never know it. He starves the fire and smothers it with wet ashes, he makes himself the cave where he sits on cold ground gnawing bones. Women's bones.

But Mollie is a brand snatched from his burning. I miss Mollie. Next time we're over east again I'll go up to Pendleton and see her and the grandbabies. She doesn't come. Never did like the way Ether ranges. She's a stayputter. Says all the moving around would make the children insecure. It didn't make her insecure in any harmful way that I can see. It's her Eric that would disapprove. He's a snob. Prison clerk. What a job. Walk out of a place every night where the others are all locked in, how's that for a ball and chain? Sink you if you ever tried to swim.

Where did Ady swim up from I wonder? Somewhere deep. Once he said he was Greek, once he said he worked on a Australian ship, once he said he had lived on an island in the Philippines where they speak a language nobody else anywhere speaks, once he said he was born in a canoe at sea. It could all have been true. Or not. Maybe Archie should go to sea. Join the Navy or the Coast Guard. But no, he'd drown.

Tad knows he'll never drown. He's Ady's son, he can breathe water. I wonder where Tad is now. That is a tugging too, that not knowing, not knowing where the child is, an aching pull you stop noticing because it never stops. But sometimes it turns you, you find you're facing another direction, like your body was caught by the thorn of a blackberry, by an undertow. The way the moon pulls the tides.

I keep thinking about Archie, I keep thinking about Needless. Ever since I saw him look at Sook. I know what it is, it's that other dream I had. Right after the one with Archie. I dreamed something, it's hard to get hold of, something about being on this long long beach, like I was beached, yes, that's it, I was stranded, and I couldn't move. I was drying up and I couldn't get back to the water. Then I saw somebody walking towards me from way far away down the beach. His tracks in the sand were ahead of him. Each time he stepped in one, in the footprint, it was gone when he lifted his foot. He kept coming straight to me and I knew if he got to me I could get back in the water and be all right. When he got close up I saw it was him. It was Needless. That's an odd dream.

If Archie went to sea he'd drown. He's a drylander, like his father.

Sookie, now, Sook is Toby Walker's daughter. She knows it. She told me, once, I didn't tell her. Sook goes her own way. I don't know if he knows it. I don't think so. She has my eyes and hair. And there were some other possibilities. And I never felt it was the right thing to tell a man unless he asked. Toby didn't ask, because of what he believed about himself. But I knew the night, I knew the moment she was conceived. I felt the child to be leap in me like a fish leaping in the sea, a salmon coming up the river, leaping the rocks and rapids, shining. Toby had told me he couldn't have children—"not with any woman born," he said, with a sorrowful look. He came pretty near telling me where he came from, that night. But I didn't ask. Maybe because of what I believe about myself, that I only have the one life and no range, no freedom to walk in the hidden places.

Anyhow, I told him that that didn't matter, because if I felt like it I could conceive by taking thought. And for all I know that's what happened. I thought Sookie and out she came, red as a salmon, quick and shining. She is the most beautiful child, girl, woman. What does she want to stay here in Ether for? Be an old maid teacher like Emma? Pump gas, give perms, clerk in the grocery? Who'll she meet here? Well, God knows I met enough. I like it, she says, I like not knowing where I'll wake up. She's like me. But still there's the tug, the dry longing. Oh, I guess I had too many children. I turn this way, that way, like a compass with forty Norths. Yet always going on the same way in the end. Fitting my feet into my footprints that disappear behind me.

It's a long way down from the mountains. My feet hurt.

Tobinye Walker

Man is the animal that binds time, they say. I wonder. We're bound by time, bounded by it. We move from a place to another place, but from a time to another time only in memory and intention, dream and prophecy. Yet time travels us. Uses us as its road, going on never stopping always in one direction. No exits off this freeway.

I say *we* because I am a naturalized citizen. I didn't use to be a citizen at all. Time once was to me what my back yard is to Emma's cat. No fences mattered, no boundaries. But I was forced to stop, to settle, to join. I am an American. I am a castaway. I came to grief.

I admit I've wondered if it's my doing that Ether ranges, doesn't stay put. An effect of my accident. When I lost the power to walk straight, did I impart a twist to the locality? Did it begin to travel because my travelling had ceased? If so, I can't work out the mechanics of it. It's logical, it's neat, yet I don't think it's the fact. Perhaps I'm just dodging my responsibility. But to the best of my memory, ever since Ether was a town it's always been a real American town, a place that isn't where you left it. Even when you live there it isn't where you think it is. It's missing. It's restless. It's off somewhere over the mountains, making up in one dimension what it lacks in another. If it doesn't keep moving the malls will catch it. Nobody's surprised it's gone. The white man's his own burden. And nowhere to lay it down. You can leave town easy enough, but coming back is tricky. You come back to where you left it and there's nothing but the parking lot for the new mall and a giant yellow grinning clown made of balloons. Is that all there was to it? Better not believe it, or that's all you'll ever have: blacktop and cinderblock and a blurred photograph of a little boy smiling. The child was murdered along with many others. There's more to it than that, there is an old glory in it, but it's hard to locate, except by accident. Only Roger Hiddenstone can come back when he wants to, riding his old Ford or his old horse, because Roger owns nothing but the desert and a true heart. And of course wherever Edna is, it is. It's where she lives.

I'll make my prophecy. When Starra and Roger lie in each

other's tender arms, she sixteen he sixty, when Gracie and Archie shake his pickup truck to pieces making love on the mattress in the back on the road out to the Hohovars, when Ervin Muth and Thomas Sunn get drunk with the farmers in the ashram and dance and sing and cry all night, when Emma Bodely and Pearl Amethyst gaze long into each other's shining eyes among the cats, among the crystals—that same night Needless the grocer will come at last to Edna. To him she will bear no child but joy. And orange trees will blossom in the streets of Ether.

Unlocking the Air

This is a fairy tale. People stand in the lightly falling snow. Something is shining, trembling, making a silvery sound. Eyes are shining. Voices sing. People laugh and weep, clasp one another's hands, embrace. Something shines and trembles. They live happily ever after. The snow falls on the roofs and blows across the parks, the squares, the river.

This is history. Once upon a time a good king lived in his palace in a kingdom far away. But an evil enchantment fell upon that land. The wheat withered in the ear, the leaves dropped from the trees of the forest, and no thing thrived.

This is a stone. It's a paving stone of a square that slants downhill in front of an old, reddish, almost windowless fortress called the Roukh Palace. The square was paved nearly three hundred years ago, so a lot of feet have walked on this stone, bare feet and shod, children's little pads, horses' iron shoes, soldiers' boots; and wheels have gone over and over it, cart wheels, carriage wheels, car tires, tank treads. Dogs' paws every now and then. There's been dogshit on it, there's been blood, both soon washed away by water sloshed from buckets or run from hoses or dropped from the clouds. You can't get blood from a stone, they say, nor can you give it to a stone; it takes no stain. Some of the pavement, down near that street that leads out of Roukh Square through the old Jewish quarter to the river, got dug up once or twice and piled into a barricade, and some of the stones even found themselves flying through the air, but not for long. They were soon put back in their place, or replaced by others. It made no difference to them. The man hit by the flying stone dropped down like a stone beside the stone that killed him. The man shot through the brain fell down and his blood ran out on this stone, or another one maybe, it makes no difference to them. The soldiers washed his blood away with water sloshed from buckets, the buckets their horses drank from. The rain fell after a while. The snow fell. Bells rang the hours, the Christmases, the New Years. A tank stopped with its treads on this stone. You'd think that that would leave a mark, a huge heavy thing like a tank, but the stone shows nothing. Only all the feet bare and shod over the centuries have worn a quality into it, not a smoothness exactly but a kind of softness like leather or like skin. Unstained, unmarked, indifferent, it does have that quality of having been worn for a long time by life. So it is a stone of power, and who sets foot on it may be transformed.

This is a story. She let herself in with her key and called, "Mama? It's me, Fana," and her mother in the kitchen of the apartment called, "I'm in here," and they met and hugged in the doorway of the kitchen.

"Come on, come on!"

"Come where?"

"It's Thursday, Mama!"

"Oh," said Bruna Fabbre, retreating towards the stove, making vague protective gestures at the saucepans, the dishcloths, the spoons.

"You said."

"But it's nearly four already—"

"We can be back by six-thirty."

"I have all the papers to read for the advancement tests."

"You have to come, Mama. You do. You'll see!"

A heart of stone might resist the shining eyes, the coaxing, the bossiness. "Come on!" she said again, and the mother came.

But grumbling. "This is for you," she said on the stairs.

On the bus she said it again. "This is for you. Not me."

"What makes you think that?"

Bruna did not reply for a while, looking out the bus window at the grey city lurching by, the dead November sky behind the roofs.

"Well, you see," she said, "before Kasi, my brother Kasimir, before he was killed, that was the time that would have been for me. But I was too young. Too stupid. And then they killed Kasi."

"By mistake."

"It wasn't a mistake. They were hunting for a man who'd been getting people out across the border, and they'd missed him. So it was to . . ."

"To have something to report to the Central Office."

Bruna nodded. "He was about the age you are now," she said. The bus stopped, people climbed on, crowding the aisle. "Since then, twenty-seven years, always since then it's been too late. For me. First too stupid, then too late. This time is for you. I missed mine."

"You'll see," Stefana said. "There's enough time to go round."

This is history. Soldiers stand in a row before the reddish, almost windowless palace; their muskets are at the ready. Young men walk across the stones towards them, singing,

> Beyond this darkness is the light,
> O Liberty, of thine eternal day!

The soldiers fire their guns. The young men live happily ever after.

* * *

This is biology.

"Where the hell is everybody?"

"It's Thursday," Stefan Fabbre said, adding, "Damn!" as the figures on the computer screen jumped and flickered. He was wearing his topcoat over sweater and scarf, since the biology laboratory was heated only by a spaceheater which shorted out the computer circuit if they were on at the same time. "There are programs that could do this in two seconds," he said, jabbing morosely at the keyboard.

Avelin came up and glanced at the screen. "What is it?"

"The RNA comparison count. I could do it faster on my fingers."

Avelin, a bald, spruce, pale, dark-eyed man of forty, roamed the laboratory, looked restlessly through a folder of reports. "Can't run a university with this going on," he said. "I'd have thought you'd be down there."

Fabbre entered a new set of figures and said, "Why?"

"You're an idealist."

"Am I?" Fabbre leaned back, stretched, rolled his head to get the cricks out. "I try hard not to be," he said.

"Realists are born, not made." The younger man sat down on a lab stool and stared at the scarred, stained counter. "It's coming apart," he said.

"You think so? Seriously?"

Avelin nodded. "You heard that report from Prague."

Fabbre nodded.

"Last week . . . This week . . . Next year—Yes. An earthquake. The stones come apart—it falls apart—there was a building, now there's not. History is made. So I don't understand why you're here, not there."

"Seriously, you don't understand that?"

Avelin smiled and said, "Seriously."

"All right." Fabbre stood up and began walking up and down

the long room as he spoke. He was a slight, grey-haired man with youthfully intense, controlled movements. "Science or political activity, either/or: choose. Right? Choice is responsibility, right? So I chose my responsibility responsibly. I chose science and abjured all action but the acts of science. The acts of a responsible science. Out there they can change the rules; in here they can't change the rules; when they try to I resist. This is my resistance." He slapped the laboratory bench as he turned round. "I'm lecturing. I walk up and down like this when I lecture. So. Background of the choice. I'm from the northeast. '56, in the northeast, do you remember? My grandfather, my father—reprisals. So, in '60, I come here, to the university. '62, my best friend, my wife's brother. We were walking through a village market, talking, then he stopped, he stopped talking, they had shot him. A kind of mistake. Right? He was a musician. A realist. I felt that I owed it to him, that I owed it to them, you see, to live carefully, with responsibility, to do the best I could do. The best I could do was this," and he gestured around the laboratory. "I'm good at it. So I go on trying to be a realist. As far as possible under the circumstances, which have less and less to do with reality. But they are only circumstances. The circumstances in which I do my work as carefully as I can."

Avelin sat on the lab stool, his head bowed. When Fabbre was done, he nodded. After a while he said, "But I have to ask you if it's realistic to separate the circumstances, as you put it, from the work."

"About as realistic as separating the body from the mind," Fabbre said. He stretched again and reseated himself at the computer. "I want to get this series in," he said, and his hands went to the keyboard and his gaze to the notes he was copying. After five or six minutes he started the printer and spoke without turning. "You're serious, Givan, you think it's coming apart as a whole?"

"Yes. I think the experiment is over."

The printer scraped and screeched, and they raised their voices to be heard over it.

"Here, you mean."

"Here and everywhere. They know it, down at Roukh Square. Go down there. You'll see. There could be such jubilation only at the death of a tyrant or the failure of a great hope."

"Or both."

"Or both," Avelin agreed.

The paper jammed in the printer, and Fabbre opened the machine to free it. His hands were shaking. Avelin, spruce and cool, hands behind his back, strolled over, looked, reached in, disengaged the corner that was jamming the feed.

"Soon," he said, "we'll have an IBM. A Mactoshin. Our hearts' desire."

"Macintosh," Fabbre said.

"Everything can be done in two seconds."

Fabbre restarted the printer and looked around. "Listen, the principles—"

Avelin's eyes shone strangely, as if full of tears; he shook his head. "So much depends on the circumstances," he said.

This is a key. It locks and unlocks a door, the door to Apartment 2-1 of the building at 43 Pradinestrade in the Old North Quarter of the city of Krasnoy. The apartment is enviable, having a kitchen with saucepans, dishcloths, spoons, and all that is necessary, and two bedrooms, one of which is now used as a sitting room with chairs, books, papers, and all that is necessary, as well as a view from the window between other buildings of a short section of the Molsen River. The river at this moment is lead-colored and the trees above it are bare and black. The apartment is unlighted and empty. When they left, Bruna Fabbre locked the door and dropped the key, which is on a steel ring along with the key to her desk at the Lyceum and the key to her sister Bendika's apartment in the Trasfiuve, into her small imitation leather handbag, which is getting shabby at the corners, and snapped the handbag shut. Bruna's daughter Stefana has a copy of the key in her jeans pocket, tied on a bit of braided cord along with the key to the closet in her room in Dormitory G of the University of Krasnoy, where she is a graduate student in the department of Orsinian and Slavic Literature working for a degree in the field of Early Romantic Poetry. She never locks the closet. The two women walk down Pradinestrade three blocks and wait a few minutes at the corner for the number 18 bus, which runs on Bulvard Settentre from North Krasnoy to the center of the city.

Pressed in the crowded interior of the handbag and the tight warmth of the jeans pocket, the key and its copy are inert, silent, forgotten. All a key can do is lock and unlock its door; that's all the function it has, all the meaning; it has a responsibility but no rights. It can lock or unlock. It can be found or thrown away.

This is history. Once upon a time in 1830, in 1848, in 1866, in 1918, in 1947, in 1956, stones flew. Stones flew through the air like pigeons, and hearts, too, hearts had wings. Those were the years when the stones flew, the hearts took wing, the young voices sang. The soldiers raised their muskets to the ready, the soldiers aimed their rifles, the soldiers poised their machine guns. They were young, the soldiers. They fired. The stones lay down, the pigeons fell. There's a kind of red stone called pigeon's blood, a ruby. The red stones of Roukh Square were never rubies; slosh a bucket of water over them or let the rain fall and they're grey again, lead grey, common stones. Only now and then in certain years they have flown, and turned to rubies.

This is a bus. Nothing to do with fairy tales and not romantic; certainly realistic; though in a way, in principle, in fact, it is highly idealistic. A city bus crowded with people in a city street in Central Europe on a November afternoon, and it's stalled. What else? Oh, dear. Oh, damn. But no, it hasn't stalled; the engine, for a wonder, hasn't broken down; it's just that it can't go any farther. Why not? Because there's a bus stopped in front of it, and another one stopped in front of that one at the cross street, and it looks like everything's stopped. Nobody on this bus has yet heard the word "gridlock," the name of an exotic disease of the mysterious West. There aren't enough private cars in Krasnoy to bring about a gridlock even if they knew what it was. There are cars, and a lot of wheezing idealistic busses, but all there is enough of to stop the flow of traffic in Krasnoy is people. It is a kind of equation, proved by experiments conducted over many years, perhaps not in a wholly scientific or objective spirit but nonetheless presenting a well-documented result confirmed by repetition: there are not enough people in this city to stop a tank. Even in much larger cities it has been authoritatively demonstrated as recently as last spring that there are not enough people to stop a tank. But there are enough people in this city to stop a bus, and they are doing so. Not by throwing themselves in front of it, waving banners, or singing songs about Liberty's eternal day, but merely by being in the street getting in the way of the bus, on the supposition that the bus driver has not been trained in either homicide or suicide; and on the same supposition—upon which all cities stand or fall—they are also getting in the way of all the other busses and all the cars and in one another's way, too, so that nobody is going much of anywhere, in a physical sense.

"We're going to have to walk from here," Stefana said, and her mother clutched her imitation leather handbag. "Oh, but we can't, Fana. Look at that crowd! What are they—Are they—?"

"It's Thursday, ma'am," said a large, red-faced, smiling man just behind them in the aisle. Everybody was getting off the bus, pushing and talking. "Yesterday I got four blocks closer than this," a woman said crossly, and the red-faced man said, "Ah, but this is Thursday."

"Fifteen thousand last time," said somebody, and somebody else said, "Fifty, fifty thousand today!"

"We can never get anywhere near the Square, I don't think we should try," Bruna told her daughter as they squeezed into the crowd outside the bus door.

"You stay with me, don't let go, and don't worry," said the student of Early Romantic Poetry, a tall, resolute young woman, and she took her mother's hand in a firm grasp. "It doesn't really matter where we get, but it would be fun if you could see the Square. Let's try. Let's go round behind the post office."

Everybody was trying to go the same direction. Stefana and Bruna got across one street by dodging and stopping and pushing gently; then turning against the flow they trotted down a nearly empty alley, cut across the cobbled court back of the Central Post Office, and rejoined an even thicker crowd moving slowly down a wide street and out from between the buildings. "There, there's the palace, see!" said Stefana, who could see it, being taller. "This is as far as we'll get except by osmosis." They practised osmosis, which necessitated letting go of each other's hands, and made Bruna unhappy. "This is far enough, this is fine here," she kept saying. "I can see everything. There's the roof of the palace. Nothing's going to happen, is it? I mean, will anybody speak?" It was not what she meant, but she did not want to shame her daughter with her fear, her daughter who had not been alive when the stones turned to rubies. And she spoke quietly because although there were so many people pressed and pressing into Roukh Square, they were not noisy. They talked to one another in ordinary, quiet voices. Only now and then somebody down nearer the palace shouted out a name, and then many, many other voices would repeat it with a roll and crash like a wave breaking. Then they would be quiet again, murmuring vastly, like the sea between big waves.

The street lights had come on. Roukh Square was sparsely lighted by tall, old, cast-iron standards with double globes that shed a soft light high in the air. Through that serene light, which seemed to darken the sky, came drifting small, dry flecks of snow.

The flecks melted to droplets on Stefana's dark, short hair and on the scarf Bruna had tied over her fair, short hair to keep her ears warm.

When Stefana stopped at last, Bruna stood up as tall as she could, and because they were standing on the highest edge of the Square, in front of the old Dispensary, by craning she could see the great crowd, the faces like snowflakes, countless. She saw the evening darkening, the snow falling, and no way out, and no way home. She was lost in the forest. The palace, whose few lighted windows shone dully above the crowd, was silent. No one came out, no one went in. It was the seat of government; it held the power. It was the powerhouse, the powder magazine, the bomb. Power had been compressed, jammed into those old reddish walls, packed and forced into them over years, over centuries, till if it exploded it would burst with horrible violence, hurling pointed shards of stone. And out here in the twilight in the open there was nothing but soft faces with shining eyes, soft little breasts and stomachs and thighs protected only by bits of cloth.

She looked down at her feet on the pavement. They were cold. She would have worn her boots if she had thought it was going to snow, if Fana hadn't hurried her so. She felt cold, lost, lonely to the point of tears. She set her jaw and set her lips and stood firm on her cold feet on the cold stone.

There was a sound, sparse, sparkling, faint, like the snow crystals. The crowd had gone quite silent, swept by low laughing murmurs, and through the silence ran that small, discontinuous, silvery sound.

"What is that?" asked Bruna, beginning to smile. "Why are they doing that?"

This is a committee meeting. Surely you don't want me to describe a committee meeting? It meets as usual on Friday at eleven in the morning in the basement of the Economics Building. At eleven on Friday night, however, it is still meeting, and there are a good many onlookers, several million in fact, thanks to the foreigner with the camera, a television camera with a long snout, a one-eyed snout that peers and sucks up what it sees. The cameraman focusses for a long time on the tall, dark-haired girl who speaks so eloquently in favor of a certain decision concerning bringing a certain man back to the capital. But the millions of onlookers will not understand her argument, which is spoken in her obscure language and is not translated for them. All they will know is how the eye-snout of the camera lingered on her young face, sucking it.

This is a love story. Two hours later the cameraman was long gone but the committee was still meeting.

"No, listen," she said, "seriously, this is the moment when the betrayal is always made. Free elections, yes, but if we don't look past that now, when will we? And who'll do it? Are we a country or a client state changing patrons?"

"You have to go one step at a time, consolidating—"

"When the dam breaks? You have to shoot the rapids! All at once!"

"It's a matter of choosing direction—"

"Exactly, direction. Not being carried senselessly by events."

"But all the events are sweeping in one direction."

"They always do. Back! You'll see!"

"Sweeping to what, to dependence on the West instead of the East, like Fana said?"

"Dependence is inevitable—realignment, but not occupation—"

"The hell it won't be occupation! Occupation by money, materialism, their markets, their values, you don't think we can hold out against them, do you? What's social justice to a color TV set? That battle's lost before it's fought. Where do we stand?"

"Where we always stood. In an absolutely untenable position."

"He's right. Seriously, we are exactly where we always were. Nobody else is. We are. They have caught up with us, for a moment, for this moment, and so we can act. The untenable position is the center of power. Now. We can act *now*."

"To prevent color-TV-zation? How? The dam's broken! The goodies come flooding in. And we drown in them."

"Not if we establish the direction, the true direction, right now—"

"But will Rege listen to us? Why are we turning back when we should be going forward? If we—"

"We have to establish—"

"No! We have to act! Freedom can be established only in the moment of freedom—"

They were all shouting at once in their hoarse, worn-out voices. They had all been talking and listening and drinking bad coffee and living for days, for weeks, on love. Yes, on love; these are lovers' quarrels. It is for love that he pleads, it is for love that she rages. It was always for love. That's why the camera snout came poking and sucking into this dirty basement room where the lovers meet. It craves love, the sight of love; for if you can't have the real thing you can watch it on TV, and soon you don't know the real thing from the images on the little screen where everything, as he said, can be done in two seconds. But the lovers know the difference.

This is a fairy tale, and you know that in the fairy tale, after it says that they lived happily ever after, there is no after. The evil enchantment was broken; the good servant received half the kingdom as his reward; the king ruled long and well. Remember the moment when the betrayal is made, and ask no questions. Do not ask if the poisoned fields grew white again with grain. Do not ask if the leaves of the forests grew green that spring. Do not ask what the maiden received as her reward. Remember the tale of Koshchey the Deathless, whose life was in a needle, and the needle was in an egg, and the egg was in a swan, and the swan was in an eagle, and the eagle was in a wolf, and the wolf was in the palace whose walls were built of the stones of power. Enchantment within enchantment! We are a long way yet from the egg that holds the needle that must be broken so that Koshchey the Deathless can die. And so the tale ends. Thousands and thousands and thousands of people stood on the slanting pavement before the palace. Snow sparkled in the air, and the people sang. You know the song, that old song with words like "land," "love," "free," in the language you have known the longest. Its words make stone part from stone, its words prevent tanks, its words transform the world, when it is sung at the right time by the right people, after enough people have died for singing it.

A thousand doors opened in the walls of the palace. The soldiers laid down their arms and sang. The evil enchantment was broken. The good king returned to his kingdom, and the people danced for joy on the stones of the city streets.

And we do not ask what happened after. But we can tell the story over, we can tell the story till we get it right.

"My daughter's on the Committee of the Student Action Council," said Stefan Fabbre to his neighbor Florens Aske as they stood in a line outside the bakery on Pradinestrade. His tone of voice was complicated.

"I know. Erreskar saw her on the television," Aske said.

"She says they've decided that bringing Rege here is the only way to provide an immediate, credible transition. They think the army will accept him."

They shuffled forward a step.

Aske, an old man with a hard brown face and narrow eyes, stuck his lips out, thinking it over.

"You were in the Rege Government," Fabbre said.

Aske nodded. "Minister of Education for a week," he said, and gave a bark like a sea lion, owp!—a cough or a laugh.

"Do you think he can pull it off?"

Aske pulled his grubby muffler closer round his neck and said, "Well, Rege is not stupid. But he's old. What about that scientist, that physicist fellow?"

"Rochoy. She says their idea is that Rege's brought in first, for the transition, for the symbolism, the link to '56, right? And if he survives, Rochoy would be the one they'd run in an election."

"The dream of the election . . ."

They shuffled forward again. They were now in front of the bakery window, only eight or ten people away from the door.

"Why do they put up the old men?" asked the old man. "These boys and girls, these young people. What the devil do they want us for again?"

"I don't know," Fabbre said. "I keep thinking they know what they're doing. She had me down there, you know, made me come to one of their meetings. She came to the lab—Come on, leave that, follow me! I did. No questions. She's in charge. All of them, twenty-two, twenty-three, they're in charge. In power. Seeking structure, order, but very definite: violence is defeat, to them, violence is the loss of options. They're absolutely certain and completely ignorant. Like spring—like the lambs in spring. They have never done anything and they know exactly what to do."

"Stefan," said his wife, Bruna, who had been standing at his elbow for several sentences, "you're lecturing. Hello, dear. Hello, Florens, I just saw Margarita at the market, we were queueing for cabbages. I'm on my way downtown, Stefan. I'll be back, I don't know, sometime after seven, maybe."

"Again?" he said, and Aske said, "Downtown?"

"It's Thursday," Bruna said, and bringing up the keys from her handbag, the two apartment keys and the desk key, she shook them in the air before the men's faces, making a silvery jingle; and she smiled.

"I'll come," said Stefan Fabbre.

"Owp! owp!" went Aske. "Oh, hell, I'll come too. Does man live by bread alone?"

"Will Margarita worry where you are?" Bruna asked as they left the bakery line and set off towards the bus stop.

"That's the problem with the women, you see," said the old

man, "they worry that she'll worry. Yes. She will. And you worry about your daughter, eh, your Fana."

"Yes," Stefan said, "I do."

"No," Bruna said, "I don't. I fear her, I fear for her, I honor her. She gave me the keys." She clutched her imitation leather handbag tight between her arm and side as they walked.

This is the truth. They stood on the stones in the lightly falling snow and listened to the silvery, trembling sound of thousands of keys being shaken, unlocking the air, once upon a time.

A CHILD BRIDE

Did he take me away from her or did she make me leave him? I don't know if what came first was the light. I don't know where my home was. I remember the dark car. Long, and large, and so fast that the road broke like a wave. There was the smell of the car and the smell of the sod, a cleft, an opening. The road went down, I know. What flowers smell like sometimes I remember. In the name of the hyacinth I find the colors purple, pink, red, and the color of pomegranate. But there is a forbidden color. If I say its name the punishment will come upon me, the breaking, the terrible calling, if I say the name of milk the earth will ache. The earth will ache and reach for me again, white arms and brown arms groping and grasping, seeking, choking. If I was there, under his roof, was it wrong that I was there? Was I not wanted there? I was chosen, I was queen. The arms reached out but they couldn't catch me. I didn't look up as we drove by the long, black rivers. The car went so fast by the rivers! But we would stop for me to name the rivers: Memory that carries remembering away, and Anger that runs so gently smoothing the pebbles round, and Terror that we swam in fearlessly. And then the waterfalls! I gave them no names. They are still falling down and down from deep to deeper dark till the last glimmering is lost and only the long voice of water comes back from below saying what we cannot say. Sound is a slower traveller than light, and so more sure. It was the calling that came to me from the high places, never the light. How could the light come here within? this is no place for light. It's too heavy here. But in the calling came the hyacinth, the colors that come before the light. O Mother! Mother! Mother! Who called? Who called her? me?

He's rich, Mother. He lives there in the basement of the old house with old things, dried things, roots and coins and chests and closets and shadows. He lives down in the cellar, but he's rich. He could buy anything.

No, he didn't hurt me only once. When I was frightened when he came when I was there alone. He took me away then he made me go down inside. We went inside where I had never been and I was there then. Yes, when my mother's working I always stay alone. I stay in the house and garden, where else is there to go? No, I don't know my daddy. Yes no I don't know. I don't know what it means. He made me come with him in the car. I went with him. Yes he touched me there. Yes he did that. Yes he did that. Yes we did that. Yes I said no I didn't say. He said I was his wife. He said everything he had was mine. Can I see my mother now?

Yes he gave me jewelry. I took it yes. I wore it yes. It was beautiful, the stones, amethyst, rose amethyst, ruby. He gave me the crown of hyacinth, of pomegranate stone. He gave me the ring of gold I wear. We never left the basement no. He said it was dangerous outside. He said there was a war. He said there were enemies. He never hurt me only at the start. He needed me. We did that yes I am his wife. With him I rule that place. With him I judge you all. To whom do you think you come?

She came to me and came back to me, the musician's wife, my friend. I knew she would come back. She came back crying. I knew she would. I was waiting for her by the road and cried with her when she came back alone, but not for long. Here tears dry away. Here in the dark no mourning is. A few tears, like pomegranate seeds, five or six little half-transparent seeds that look like uncut rubies, that's enough, enough to eat, enough.

O Mother don't cry, I was only playing hide and seek! I only hid! I was joking, Mother, I didn't mean to stay so long. I didn't know it was so late. I didn't notice it was dark. We were playing kings and queens and hide and seek and I didn't know, I didn't know, I didn't know. Do I live there? Is this my home? This is outside the earth and I have lived inside. This is inside the earth and I have lived outside. This is dark and I come from the light, from the dark into this light. He loves me well. He waits for me. Why is your love winter, Mother? Why are his hands so cold?

What does my mother do? She keeps the house.

There is no river long enough to wear her anger down. She will never forget and will always be afraid. You have made an enemy indeed, my lord.

Mother, be comforted. Don't cry and make me cry. Come winter I'll come back and spring is my return. I'll bring the hyacinths. You can depend on me, you know, I'm not a child now. But if I am your daughter how can I be his wife? How can I be your wife when I am her daughter? What do you want of me, who sleep in my arms? These are her arms around me rocking me, rocking me. I wear the ring of gold he gave me as I walk in the garden she grew for me, the red flowers, the purple flowers, the pomegranate trees with roots of white and brown that reach down deep. To be sought forever, but shall I be found and never seek myself and never find? To be one body root and flower, to break the sod, to drive the dark car home, to turn, return, where is my home? Shall I bear no daughter?

CLIMBING TO THE MOON

Little Aby will help her build the fire, running down from the dunes, his curly head like a thistledown-puff against the long gold light in the west. "Let's get the fire laid before it gets dark, Aby!" she'll say, and the child, eager to do grown-up work, to be her partner, to build the beautiful, dangerous fire against the fall of night, will say, "I'll get the wood!" and be off like an erratic, fuzzy-feathered arrow. He will search, stoop, and gather, rush back dropping bits of driftwood, dump his tiny load, and be off again. She will gather methodically. There are plenty of useful pieces of driftwood near the big, half-buried, half-burned log she has chosen as backlog and windbreak. Once she has her woodpile, she will begin to lean sticks up against the charred monster, over the hollow where she has arranged a tight-crumpled sheet of newspaper and bits of fine kindling. It won't be a big blaze. Huge, flaring bonfires that roar and volley out sparks are frightening to Aby, and to her too. It will be a small, bright, clear fire in this vast, clear, bright evening.

Aby will come up breathless with a "very big log"—a branch three feet long at least, and so heavy he has to drag it. She will praise the wood and the woodsman. Kneeling, putting her bare arm round his thin shoulders, she'll say, "Aby, love, look," and they'll look into the west.

"That's where the sun was," Aby will say, pointing to the center source of the immense, pale-pink rays of light that fan out, barely visible, in the far air suffused with gold above the sea.

"And that's the shadow of the earth." She will look up at the blue dimness that has risen from the mountains in the east to the top of the sky, just over them.

"Yeah!" says Aby, delighted with it all, and wriggles free. "Look, there's a even *bigger* log!" And he's off.

"When you come back we'll light the fire," she calls, feeling for the matches in her pocket. She sits down on the warm sand to watch the great rosy shafts of light shorten down and down into the darkening horizon. The breakers are quiet and regular, six or seven lines of them. Their huge noise all up and down the beach masks all lesser sounds except the rare cries of gulls flying late. No one else has a fire on the beach tonight. No one is walking down by the waterline.

When she first hears the drumming she thinks it is a helicopter, a Coast Guard patrol, and looks south for the black dot in the air; but her eye catches the movement nearer, down by the breakers, as she hears the drum-drum-drum of hooves on hard sand. The horse is at full gallop, the rider leans lightly forward, riding bareback—Beautiful! the double silhouette black against shining sand, the wild rhythm, the courage to ride at a gallop bareback! On to the north they go, fading into the dusk and the faint mist that hovers over the meeting of the water and the land. Oh, what a sight! She wishes he would come back, the centaur galloping between sea and sand, between daylight and the dark. And soon from the north comes the drum-drum-drum more felt than heard, and horse and rider take shape in the low mist, cantering now, lightly, easily. They slow and turn a little, and dropping into a walk come up across the sand to her. They halt. The horse raises his head and shakes it. He wears only a rope bridle with a single rein. "I saw you lighting the fire," the rider says.

She stands up; she puts her hand out to the horse, a dark bay with a blaze that gleams white in the twilight. She strokes the soft nose and reaches up to scratch under the sweaty forelock and around the roots of the big, delicate, flicking ears. The rider smiles. He vaults down from the horse's back. Like a cowboy, he simply drops the rein, and the horse nickers once and stands quiet. Oh, she knows this cowboy, this centaur, this bareback rider. "Where have you been riding?" she asks, and he answers, "Along the seacoast of Bohemia," smiling.

The fire has just caught. She adds a stout, barky branch which flares up at once. They sit down, one on each side, each seeing the other's face across the quivering flames, which seem to darken the twilight and draw it in around them.

"No," she says, "not Bohemia. Hungary. You've been riding with the Magyars again."

"All across the steppes," he says in his laughing voice, soft and resonant. "With the warrior hordes. Coming to loot the West."

"And the women follow along behind with the children and the colts and the tents and the beds. . . ."

"They light the fires. And the men turn around and come back to the fires."

"And my man comes around to my side of the fire," she says, and he does: a quiet movement, a warmth along her side, a warm arm round her shoulders. She turns to him and comes into his arms. The dark head bends to her: a long kiss, longer, deeper. Firelight webs rainbows in her lashes. The sand is warm and soft, a dark bed, an endless bed, its rumpled sheets the breakers glimmering.

Sleepy, she looks straight up into the shadow of the world and sees Vega, the star always at the top of the summer night. The linchpin, the keystone, the white thumbtack that holds the whole sky up. Oh, hello, she murmurs to the star. The spangle of the Milky Way is not yet visible, only the four stars of the Swan burning faint in the turquoise-cobalt sky.

The sand is still warm from the long day's sunlight, but not really soft. After a while you always remember, when you lie on it, that sand is stone. She sits up and gazes into the fire, then builds it up, adding a couple of long branches that can be shoved in farther as they burn, keeping it steady. Twigs flare up bright for a moment. Looking down the beach, now nearly dark, a faint blur of mist still hovering over the breakers, she imagines how the fire must look from down there at the waterline: a warm star, flickering, earthy. She wants to see it. She gets up, stretches, and walks slowly down to the wet sand. She does not look back till her bare feet feel the cold of the water. Then she turns and gazes at the fire up under the dunes.

It is very small, a little trembling brightness in the vast blur of dark blue-grey that has taken away the mountains. There is no other brightness but the stars. She shivers and runs, runs straight back up the sand, back to her fire, back to its warmth where two women sit in silence, one on each side, gazing into the flames. Their tanned, lined faces are lit ruddy and deeply shadowed. She sits down between them, a little breathless, her back to the sea.

"How's the water?" one of them asks, and she says only, "Brrr!"

"When was it we went to the beach at Santa Cruz?" the older woman asks the younger, who answers, "Right after the war. Wasn't it? I remember complaining about picnics with no hard-boiled eggs."

"Spam. Terrible stuff. Salted grease, think of it! She was just a baby. Three, maybe?"

"More like five?"

Their voices have always been quiet, never final. There is always a leaving open, a possibility of question.

"I remember we had a fire on the beach, against a driftlog, like this. We sat so late. Yes, it was then, because I remember thinking, no war out there, and it was hard to believe, after so long, that it was just the sea out there again. We were talking. She'd been asleep for ages. Curled up on the blanket. All of a sudden, out of nowhere, she said, 'Mama, will it go on forever?' Do you remember that? I never knew if she was awake or dreaming."

"We'd been trying to remember names of constellations. I remember. She must have been half awake; she was looking at the fire. 'Will it go on forever?' And you said yes. 'Yes, it will.' And she settled down again perfectly satisfied."

"Did I? Did I really? I'd forgotten. . . ." They laughed quietly, little soft grunting laughs. She looked from one face to the other: a good deal alike, though one was webbed and cragged and the other still full, with a soft underlip. The deepest eyes glinted in the firelight.

"Oh," she said, "oh but it didn't—it doesn't—Does it?"

They looked at her, four tiny warm fires glinting and trembling in their eyes. Did they laugh? They were smiling. Outside the circle of the firelight a man spoke briefly and a woman answered him. "How about another piece of wood?" one of the men said, and she looked at her fire and decided it was time for the piece she had been saving, the massive trunk-end of a large branch, perfectly dry. She laid it with care in the bright center where it would catch fast and burn hot. Sparks flew up into the air that was now quite dark. All the stars hung over the fire, over the sea. The path of the Galaxy whitened the quiet water far out beyond the breakers. Now and then a flash of light broke across the sand: luminous water, tiny sea-beings, sea-fireflies. The mist was gone, the dark was clear. The company of the stars shone brighter than the brief gleams among the breakers.

The fire creaked and crackled, and the damp core of a log hissed and sang. They all sat or lay near the flames as the night grew cooler, her people, some talking softly, others stargazing or sleeping. Aby had long been asleep, curled up on the blanket beside her. She pulled the blanket back over his bare legs. He wriggled and made a protest in his dream. "There," she murmured. "It will. Yes, it will, love." Up in the dunes one of the horses snorted. The sound of the sea was low and long and deep, a huge roar up and down the edge of the land, too large to listen to for long. Sometimes a warmer breath of wind moved seaward, smelling of soil and summer, and a few sparks flew out on it for a moment.

She got up at last, stiff. She slowly covered over the embers with cold sand. When that was done, she climbed the dunes alone in starlight towards the moon, which had not risen yet.

DADDY'S BIG GIRL

It was a terrible thing for Daddy. You can tell how hard it was on him by the fact that he's never said one word about where Jewel Ann is now. And he was the one who named her Jewel Ann instead of plain Ann like they had planned, because she was his little treasure baby. He was crazy about her when she was little.

I was six when she was born and I can remember her coming home from the hospital with Mother, and how Daddy thought the world of her. I did too. She was so little and she smelled good the way babies do, and I could help Mother take care of her, bringing diapers and getting the bath oil and powder and things. I was the first person after Mother that Jewel Ann smiled at, and I was proud of that. She was my baby too. I used to stand by her stroller and guard her when Mother was in the store. When she outgrew the stroller I was supposed to hold her hand while Mother shopped, and we always went and looked at the machines at the front of the store where they had gumballs for a penny and plastic balls with prizes inside for a dime or a quarter, curled-up snakes and jewelry and magic toys. I'd say which prizes I wished would come out if we had the quarter to put in, and Jewel Ann always chose the same ones I did. Once an old man held out a quarter to us, and I don't think he meant anything bad, but we had been taught and turned away and didn't take it. Later when we told Mother she gave us each a quarter. But when we put the money into the machine none of the plastic balls you could see came out or even moved, because there were other prizes underneath them that you couldn't see, and those were what came out. Mine was a paper American flag on like a toothpick with a sort of stand. Jewel Ann's was a pink plastic ring without even a glass diamond in it. But she was still little enough that she liked it, and she kept the plastic balls that came apart, too, and used them for tea sets and things. When we got those prizes Jewel Ann was tall enough to put her own quarter in the slot machine. She could talk as well as most grown-ups, and do all my old wooden puzzles Grandmother gave me, and when we played house she wasn't the baby any more but a lady called Mrs. Goopie, and I was Mrs. Boopie next door. We played Mrs. Goopie and Mrs. Boopie all spring after my school and all summer, in the back yard under the pines, with our dolls for the children. Duane never played with us, only the kind of games where you win or lose, with other boys. None of the girls I knew at school lived anywhere near us, because of bussing, and I didn't know the girls in our neighborhood very well. Anyhow I liked playing with Jewel Ann better because she was smart, and even if she was younger she was bigger than me by the time she was five so it wasn't like she was so much younger. And anyhow I did love her, and she loved me back.

The first day she went to school I took her on the bus and showed her where everything was at school and went with her to the first grade room. The teacher said, "My, Jewel Ann, you are tall!" She said it not in a nice way but like it was Jewel Ann's fault. Then she said to me the same way, "Is she really only five?"

I said, "Yes, Mrs. Hanlan."

She said, "She's far too big for a girl of five. It will be very difficult for the little boys."

Jewel Ann said, "I'll be six next year!" She was trying to help.

But Mrs. Hanlan acted like she thought she was showing off, and told her to go sit down. When Jewel Ann sat down on the little chair in the circle she was still as tall as the other first graders standing up. It made me feel funny for her, after what Mrs. Hanlan had said. But Jewel Ann smiled and waved at me, because she was so excited about going to school and wanted it to begin.

She always did real well in her work, and had a perfect attendance record, and when she was in the third grade Miss Shulz made her a monitor and gave her advanced reading books and put her painting of whales in the Save the Animals poster contest. It got Honorable Mention. Jewel Ann was happy that year. But then they kept her out of school the next fall because of her height, and she never got to go back.

I knew she was tall but I hadn't really noticed till practically that first day at her first grade. I mean, I knew, but I didn't have to compare her to anybody till then. And she was still my little sister. I don't know when Daddy stopped calling her "Daddy's big girl," I guess when she was around three. I don't think they tried to do anything about it until that summer after she was in third grade. She had been growing a lot, and Daddy made Mother take her to a doctor. Mother told me about it later. They gave her some hormones. Mother threw them out after a week because they made Jewel Ann get dizzy and have headaches and throw up, and also Mother was afraid that if she went on taking them the hormones would cause her to have periods or grow a beard. She was only a little girl of eight, and Mother felt it wasn't right. I guess she didn't tell Daddy and he went on thinking Jewel Ann had taken all those hormones and it had cost a lot and done no good. Anyhow he never mentioned sending her to the doctors again. Mother said she knew it wasn't going to do any good. It wasn't hormones in the first place.

Jewel Ann didn't cry about not going back to school, but she stopped talking about Miss Shulz. I don't know what she thought. She was quiet. Like I said, she had been happy in Miss Shulz's room, but there were always some people at school who picked on her. At home nobody was mean to her except Duane. He called her names like Giraffe and Hugie and Flagpole, and said things like, "When are you going to sell her to the freak show?" and worse. Once I heard him talking with his friend Eddie and saying he wished he could kill Jewel Ann. He said, "Chop her all apart into little bits, fry her with one of those flame-throwers, just burn her down into nothing." It embarrassed Duane that she was so tall that she could look down on the top of his head when she was eight years old and he was sixteen. He was just average height for his age, like me. I think Jewel Ann getting so tall was partly why Duane went so wild in his teens. But not entirely. He never had been goodnatured that I can remember. Anyhow he got wilder and meaner, and Daddy was always yelling at him until he went off to Atlanta and we don't know where after that. A couple of years later when the newspaper article came out somebody must have showed it to him, because he sent a letter the next month to Mother and Daddy saying that he had a friend who was interested in making movies with unusual people in them and there could be a lot of money in it for us. The postmark was Fort Worth but there was no return address and the letter was hard to read, like he spelled unusual "sunual," and his writing was funny. Mother cried a couple of times after that letter came, but I don't think she was really missing Duane. It was thinking about him sometimes when he was a baby that made her cry.

I brought books and stuff from school for a year for Jewel Ann but the next year they told me not to. I guess Daddy had told them that she was in a special school. He had built up the back yard fence and Jewel Ann could play outside. But around her twelfth birthday she really began getting her growth, and that was when the newspaper people came. We were washing dishes and heard Daddy talking at the front door with somebody. We listened because he didn't have any friends that ever came to the house and we wondered who it was. Then he came into the kitchen yelling to Jewel Ann to go to her room. We had watched *The Diary of Anne Frank* on TV that week and she sort of thought it was the Nazis, and so we both ran into her room and locked the door. Jewel Ann's room was what used to be the family room, at the back of the house. Daddy had taken out its ceiling and the floor of the bedroom above it, that used to be Duane's room, so it was two stories tall, and he made the doors taller, too, for Jewel Ann. She was so scared of the Nazis now that she tried to hide under the bed. Her bed was three old bedsteads put end to end with the head and foot boards taken off, and she couldn't get under it because of the legs. So we pushed one of the beds against the door, and I was telling her there weren't any Nazis here, when we heard Daddy slam the front door and yell at Mother, "Don't you ever let those people come around here again!" as if she had.

Somebody had taken a picture of Jewel Ann in the back yard and sold it to the paper, and they published it with an article entitled GIRL TOPS PINES? After that Daddy cancelled our subscription to the paper, so Mother never knew about sales unless she went next door to the Heltsers' to look at their paper, and Daddy didn't know about the other article they printed after the reporter talked to me coming home from high school. She was young and really friendly, with designer clothes and a nice way of talking. It was easy to talk to her. Some of what I said came out in the *Register*, and people at school showed me the article, but when I read it it didn't sound like what I meant. Anyhow I bought a copy of the paper and brought it home for Jewel Ann so she could read about herself even if she couldn't go outside any more except after dark. It was entitled SISTER NOT HOAX, GIRL CLAIMS. It seems like nobody told Daddy about it, and we didn't show it to Mother because she was sensitive about people noticing Jewel Ann and afraid Daddy would blame her for it. But Jewel Ann liked it, especially the part that said she was an otherwise normal pre-teen with a shy smile. I don't know how the reporter actually knew that. After the articles were in the paper people used to come by and stare at the fence around the back yard, especially on Sundays when people drive around after church. Some boys probably from Cleveland High knocked at the door and when my mother came one of them said, "Is this where Jewel Ann lives?" but the others said they were at the wrong house and they all went off fooling around and laughing the gug, guh way those kind of boys do, like Duane. Mother was all confused and tight-faced when she came back to the kitchen. She said to me, "Don't you tell Jewel Ann!" I shook my head I wouldn't. Daddy was watching baseball on TV and didn't notice anything.

I think maybe Mother had really thought just at first that those boys were friends of Jewel Ann's, before she'd had time to think that they couldn't be, because a while after that while we were making a bed she said, "I do worry about Jewel Ann!"

I said, "Why?" and she said, "Well, it just is a fact that boys like girls to be shorter than they are. I don't know what to do about Jewel Ann's *social* life."

Jewel Ann and I had talked about boys, too, wondering if there were any really tall ones. It seemed to us that if there were really very tall boys you'd hear about them. Since boys are supposed to be tall, maybe their parents would be proud of them, and they could go outside and do things. It seemed to us, anyhow, that if there were enough really tall boys to be any use, we'd know about them.

So I didn't know what to say to Mother, and she didn't know what to do. Her social life wasn't so great either. She didn't go out of the house much more than Jewel Ann did. Mrs. Heltser stayed friends and sometimes she got Mother to go to the mall shopping with her, but most of the time Mother said she was so busy with the house she just couldn't take the time, and would I come by the store on the way home from school, or would I run down to the Quik-Mart after Daddy had brought the car home from work. And she ordered clothes from mail order catalogues. Except for Jewel Ann. For her clothes I bought the material and Mother designed and made them. Even bluejeans, because she wanted bluejeans so bad. Mother found the easiest way to make Jewel Ann things was to buy king-size sheets, a lot of them have nice colors and floral prints, and sew them together and then cut out the dress or the skirt and top. For the jeans I had to buy a whole bolt of jeans material. The saleswoman acted ugly and didn't want to sell me the whole bolt, as if it was wrong or something, instead of easy profit for the store, but I just stood there, and finally she flipflopped all the cloth off the center thing as if she didn't want to touch it, talking over her shoulder to another clerk all the time. Luckily Dottie Shine from high school was on the cash register and she kept the package under the counter for me, because the material was so heavy I had to come home and ask Mrs. Heltser to drive me back downtown to get it. The jeans were really hard for Mother to make, but Jewel Ann just loved them and wore them all the time.

You would have thought Jewel Ann would have eaten a lot, and there was a while I remember Daddy did criticise Mother for buying ten or twenty pounds of hamburger at a time and half a dozen heads of lettuce and so on, but actually as she grew more it seemed like all the time Jewel Ann ate less. So the grocery shopping and prices were really no big problem, especially after I finished at Coolidge High and got work in the secretary pool at Sacchi Products while I was taking computer skills at the secretarial college at night so that I would be able to earn more, which I did once I got the assistant to Mr. Penitto's executive secretary job. And it was steadier money than what Daddy could get with Shaughnessy Siding. But by then Jewel Ann wasn't eating very much at all, less than me, even less than Mother. She was fifteen years old and she was about forty-five feet tall and still growing.

If we only could have moved and lived somewhere else. If we would have had more money, or if Daddy would have been able to realise that she really was that big and really needed room, then we could have gone to live maybe by the sea somewhere, on a lonely part of the seashore or on some island where Jewel Ann could walk along the beaches and go swimming in the sea, and there would be room for her. We used to talk about that. She used to say, if she could go swimming in the sea, or walk on a beach, or walk on the moors and the heaths like Cathy Earnshaw in *Wuthering Heights* or Dimity Trescott in *Bride of Passion*. But there weren't any beaches or moors where we lived.

Jewel Ann had a hi-fi, she liked Emmy Lou Harris records, and she watched TV and read a lot. She was good at turning the pages of the books even when she could hold a book on the palm of her hand like it was a postage stamp would be on mine. I went to the library for her every week. The librarians always asked about my sister, I think they thought she was like paralysed or something, and they'd think of books for me to bring her. Once when she was about ten they gave me *Alice in Wonderland*, which was really different from the movie. Jewel Ann kept asking for it back again, so I read it once and we talked about it. I thought it was the "Drink Me" bottle she liked, with the stuff that made Alice shrink down so fast. But Jewel Ann said what she liked best was the parts with the sheep and the rushes and the forest where they forgot. I went to the bookstore in the mall and bought it for her for Christmas that year. The librarians sent her *Gulliver* once, about the little people and the giants, but she didn't like it. She said it wasn't real. In the evenings when I was home we usually watched TV together on the eighteen-inch set Daddy gave her. She said she liked TV because all the people on TV are all different sizes, but all tiny. All different sizes of tiny.

Records and TV and reading were about all she had to do, because after she was thirteen she was like Alice at the end of the first part of the book, she was too big to get out the door. If only we could have lived on a farm like Grandmother had when she was alive, and had a barn. She could have lived in a barn, I think. We used to talk about that and plan it, how I would save up and buy some old farm out in the country, and she could walk on our land at night and have a chair and things the right size for her in the barn. We talked a lot about that. We would be sitting on the floor because there wasn't anything but the carpet in her room any more, and I would lean back against her big, warm, soft leg, and we would just talk. But as time went on my sister began not to talk so much even to me.

When she outgrew her bluejeans, she felt bad. She stopped watching TV. It was like she had stopped pretending she could be like the people on TV or anywhere else. That was when she began not talking much, even though she still liked for me to come in and talk or just sit with her. She stopped reading books and she wasn't hardly eating anything. It was just very gradual for a year and more, when she was fourteen, and then fifteen, and I guess Mother and I didn't talk much about it because how could we think about it at all, really, when she was thirty-five, and forty, and forty-five feet tall? We couldn't ever talk to Daddy about it. He never said anything about her and never talked to her or went into her room, and tried to act like she wasn't even in the house, except when once he bought her some candy at Valentine's Day, and he gave her the big TV set for her birthday when she was twelve. But other times if you just said her name he'd get mad. Once when Mother and I tried to talk about maybe moving to a bigger house or something, he started yelling, and he yelled names at Mother, and broke some stuff, and finally stomped out. He didn't come back till way late at night. Mother was sick for a couple of days after that. I guess some of the things he called her were words she had heard before but never thought anybody would ever call her such things, or anyway not her own husband. She was so miserable she couldn't hear a word about moving after that, and she never went out of the house. She kept the blinds down and put paper on some of the windows. It was hard to talk about Jewel Ann even with her.

But it was her, not me, that finally said what I hadn't been able to really even think, not so as I knew I was thinking it. We were in the kitchen one night doing dishes and she said, "Dawn, I can see through her."

I didn't say anything, but in a listening way.

She said, "I could see the wallpaper where her shoulder and hair was. Through her."

I said, "I thought so too, a couple of times."

We were whispering. Except for Daddy's baseball game on TV in the front room there wasn't any other sound in the house. There wasn't ever any sound from the back room, the high room, where Jewel Ann was, sitting with her knees bent or lying on her side with her knees bent because she was too tall to stretch out any more. She was always quiet. She never had had a loud voice. Mother always used to tell us ladies don't yell, and we learned to talk softly. Now Jewel Ann hardly ever talked at all, and only in the softest voice, deep for a girl, but softer than downy feathers. And when she moved she never made a noise, though if she had stretched and pushed and wanted to she could have pushed out the back wall of that house, pushed it down like the side of a paper box. But she lay still. When I went in to sit with her that night I could see the shag carpet through her thighs and hands. Now I could see what I could see, since Mother had said it.

Jewel Ann could see it too. But we never could talk about it.

Only a couple of months after that, at the end of summer, she said once—the only thing she'd said for days, though she always touched me, even though I couldn't feel her touch any more, only like a warm breeze moving against my skin—she said, "I've stopped growing." I could tell she was smiling.

I began crying all of a sudden and saying, "Don't! Don't!"

I could feel her watching me and feel that she was warm, though I could hardly see her at all by then, only like ghosts on the TV or heat waves on blacktop, a kind of thickening in the air, but warm.

"Should I keep on?" she said in that soft feather voice.

I said, "Yes!" and couldn't stop crying. I could feel the warmness moving over my hair and arm, very lightly. She was afraid to hurt me, touching me, being so much bigger. But she never could have hurt me.

After crying so much I was worn out and fell asleep in her room that night. When I woke up early in the morning she was there, but even the TV-ghost kind of seeing her was gone. And when I said her name there was no answer.

We waited a long time, more than a week, and then Mother said, "She's gone."

She took apart the clothes made of sheets, and I took the ones from the skirt, that were whole, down to the Goodwill.

But I kept going into Jewel Ann's room, and I said, "She's still there, Mother."

Mother shook her head. She was certain. "She's gone," she said. "She's still *here*, but she's not in *there*."

And Mother was right, I guess. After a while I moved my bed into the back room, the high room, because it seemed like when I was falling asleep or beginning to wake up mornings I could feel the warmth, and then I knew Jewel Ann was there like she used to be, tall and thin and soft, with her beautiful eyes, and she was glad I was there. But then sometimes Mother hears her up in their bedroom, just saying a word or two, softly, overhead. And no matter what Daddy does to the TV and the cable, both sets always have these ghosts, and the baseball and basketball players are like you were watching with your eyes crossed. But it's outside at night I know that she's still here but gone, just like Mother said. In the back yard, warm nights when the wind blows a little and the leaves move and move, or when it's raining, then I know she didn't stop growing. I can hear her breathe.

FINDINGS

She wrote a story in the past tense. Her story told how she waited in the garden while he crossed the deserts and sailed the seas and won great victories and at last came home to her where she waited in the garden under the high green hill. "And so," the story ended, "they were married."

He wrote a story in the past tense. His story told how he sought for his father. Yearning, the young man left all who loved him, wandered through forests and cities, crossed the deserts and sailed the seas, ever seeking, ever yearning, until at last he found the lost father, and killed him. "And so," the story ended, "I came home."

She read the story. She read slowly, because the language was not her native tongue. It did not speak to her, it did not say "You." But it was a sad, beautiful story, that made her weep while she read it.

She writes a story in the present tense. It tells of the moment she sees her daughter huddled in a chair, snatching a brief rest, looking frail, with so much to do, more than her share, more than can be done. She sees her daughter is not as beautiful as she was a year ago. She writes a story of that moment, saying, "I see you worn out but willing, like a good horse, a good workhorse never biting, never kicking, never breaking free. You never can go out into the garden. You are weary to the bone at the end of every day." As she writes she wonders: Did anyone ever look at me and see me that way? Yes, she thinks, I remember the way my mother looked at me once; I think she was seeing me as I see my daughter now. But was I as weary as my daughter is? I don't know. She was more beautiful then. Was she angry? I do not know how to tell this story. It does not end with a marriage.

He writes a story in the present tense. It tells how the son leaves home to seek his father. The young man is tricked by crooks in the cities, he fights enemies, he is betrayed by faithless women, he wages war, he flies through space to other worlds, ever seeking, ever yearning, and at last he finds his father. They embrace, and the father dies. The story ends, "And so I have come home at last."

She reads his story. She reads it slowly. She wonders if she understands it. She wonders if she wants to understand it. It is a sad, beautiful story, but she does not feel like crying.

What we shall never know, he writes, is what a woman wants.

What I want, she thinks, is to write a story. But before I write the story I want to know why my mother looked at me that way. She looked at me with pity. Did she look at me with admiration? Did she look at me with rage? I look now at my daughter, that strong little woman who sits huddled in a chair for a moment before she gets up again to do more than can be done. I look at her with pity, with admiration, with rage. How beautiful she is! She is as beautiful as my mother was and her daughter will be. And so I must write her story in the second person in the future tense. It is to do with a different way of being. It is to be understood. It is to be complicated, unlike the simple, vertical singularity of the first person.

The first person singular travels all over the world, from world to world, through space and time. The first person loves and hates and seeks and kills. The first person is loved, hated, yearned for, sought for, killed. The first person is pitied. Oh, I pity myself! Just as I pity him, and as he pities himself, and as she pitied me! The first person can even be admired. Oh, how I admire myself! Just as he admires himself! But the first person cannot be raged for. I rage not for myself but for her, and she for me, in the old silence of collusion.

It is our rage that tells me how to tell the story. You will be more beautiful, I write. You will not do more than can be done. You will neither betray nor collude. I am writing the story of how you will walk in the garden under the high green hill. You will open the garden gate. You will walk up the hill and over it, across the fields, into the forests, through the cities, finding your way, finding our silences, in which you will speak.

And all the time I write, she writes, I will be at home, where you have always been. We know where to find each other.

OLDERS

The moon slips and shines in the wrinkled mirror before the prow, and from the northern sky the Bright Companions shoot glancing arrows of light along the water. In the stern of the boat the polesman stands in the watchful solemnity of his task. His movements as he poles and steers the boat are slow, certain, august. The long, low channelboat slides on the black water as silently as the reflection it pursues. A few dark figures huddle in it. One dark figure lies full length on the halfdeck, arms at his sides, closed eyes unseeing that other moon slipping and shining through wisps of fog in the luminous blue night sky. The Husbandman of Sandry is coming home from war.

They had been waiting for him on Sandry Island ever since last spring, when he went with seven men following the messengers who came to raise the Queen's army. In midsummer four of the men of Sandry brought back the news that he was wounded and was lying in the care of the Queen's own physician. They told of his great valor in battle, and told of their own prowess too, and how they had won the war. Since then there had been no news.

With him now in the channelboat were the three companions who had stayed with him, and a physician sent by the Queen, an assistant to her own doctor. This man, an active, slender person in his forties, cramped by the long night's travel, was quick to leap ashore when the boat slid silently up along the stone quay of Sandry Farm.

While the boatmen and the others busied themselves making the boat fast and lifting the stretcher and its burden up from the boat to the quay, the doctor went on up to the house. Approaching the island, as the sky imperceptibly lightened from night blue to colorless pallor, he had seen the spires of windmills, the crowns of trees, and the roofs of the house, all in black silhouette, standing very high after the miles of endlessly level reed-beds and water-channels. "Hello, the people!" he called out as he entered the courtyard. "Wake up! Sandry has come home!"

The kitchen was astir already. Lights sprang up elsewhere in the big house. The doctor heard voices, doors. A stableboy came vaulting out of the loft where he had slept, a dog barked and barked its tardy warning, people began to come out of the house-door. As the stretcher was borne into the courtyard, the Farmwife came hurrying out, wrapped in a green cloak that hid her night-dress, her hair loose, her feet bare on the stones. She ran to the stretcher as they set it down. "Farre, Farre," she said, kneeling, bending over the still figure. No one spoke or moved in that moment. "He is dead," she said in a whisper, drawing back.

"He is alive," the doctor said. And the oldest of the litterbearers, Pask the saddler, said in his rumbling bass, "He lives, Makali-dem. But the wound was deep."

The doctor looked with pity and respect at the Farmwife, at her bare feet and her clear, bewildered eyes. "Dema," he said, "let us bring him in to the warmth."

"Yes, yes," she said, rising and running ahead to prepare.

When the stretcherbearers came out again, half the people of Sandry were in the courtyard waiting to hear their news. Most of all they looked to old Pask when he came out, and he looked at them all. He was a big, slow man, girthed like an oak, with a stiff face set in deep lines. "Will he live?" a woman ventured. Pask continued looking them all over until he chose to speak. "We'll plant him," he said.

"Ah, ah!" the woman cried, and a groan and sigh went among them all.

"And our grandchildren's children will know his name," said Dyadi, Pask's wife, bosoming through the crowd to her husband. "Hello, old man."

"Hello, old woman," Pask said. They eyed each other from an equal height.

"Still walking, are you?" she said.

"How else get back where I belong?" Pask said. His mouth was too set in a straight line to smile, but his eyes glinted a little.

"Took your time doing it. Come on, old man. You must be perishing." They strode off side by side towards the lane that led to the saddlery and paddocks. The courtyard buzzed on, all in low-voiced groups around the other two returned men, getting and giving the news of the wars, the city, the marsh isles, the farm.

Indoors, in the beautiful high shadowy room where Farre now lay in the bed still warm from his wife's sleep, the physician stood by the bedside, as grave, intent, careful as the polesman had stood in the stern of the channelboat. He watched the wounded man, his fingers on the pulse. The room was perfectly still.

The woman stood at the foot of the bed, and presently he turned to her and gave a quiet nod that said, *Very well, as well as can be expected.*

"He seems scarcely to breathe," she whispered. Her eyes looked large in her face knotted and clenched with anxiety.

"He's breathing," the escort assured her. "Slow and deep. Dema, my name is Hamid, assistant to the Queen's physician, Dr. Saker. Her Majesty and the Doctor, who had your husband in his care, desired me to come with him and stay here as long as I am needed, to give what care I can. Her Majesty charged me to tell you that she is grateful for his sacrifice, that she honors his courage in her service. She will do what may be done to prove that gratitude and to show that honor. And still she bade me tell you that whatever may be done will fall short of his due."

"Thank you," said the Farmwife, perhaps only partly understanding, gazing only at the set, still face on the pillow. She was trembling a little.

"You're cold, dema," Hamid said gently and respectfully. "You should get dressed."

"Is he warm enough? Was he chilled, in the boat? I can have the fire laid—"

"No. He's warm enough. It's you I speak of, dema."

She glanced at him a little wildly, as if seeing him that moment. "Yes," she said. "Thank you."

"I'll come back in a little while," he said, laid his hand on his heart, and quietly went out, closing the massive door behind him.

He went across to the kitchen wing and demanded food and drink for a starving man, a thirsty man leg-cramped from crouching in a damned boat all night. He was not shy, and was used to the authority of his calling. It had been a long journey overland from the city, and then poling through the marshes, with Broad Isle the only hospitable place to stop among the endless channels, and the sun beating down all day, and then the long dreamlike discomfort of the night. He made much of his hunger and travail to amuse his hosts and to divert them, too, from asking questions about how the Husbandman did and would do. He did not want to tell them more than the man's wife knew.

But they, discreet or knowing or respectful, asked no direct questions of him. Though their concern for Farre was plain, they asked only, by various indirections, if he was sure to live, and seemed satisfied by that assurance. In some faces Hamid thought he saw a glimpse of something beyond satisfaction: a brooding acceptance in one; an almost conniving intelligence in another. One young fellow blurted out, "Then will he be—" and shut his mouth, under the joined stares of five or six older people.

They were a trapmouthed lot, the Sandry Islanders. All that were not actively young looked old: seamed, weatherbeaten, brown skin wrinkled and silvery, hands gnarled, hair thick, coarse, and dry. Only their eyes were quick, observant. And some of them had eyes of an unusual color, like amber: Pask, his wife Dyadi, and several others, as well as Farre himself. The first time Hamid had seen Farre, before the coma deepened, he had been struck by the strong features and those light, clear eyes. They all spoke a strong dialect, but Hamid had grown up not far inland from the marshes, and anyhow had an ear for dialects. By the end of his large and satisfying breakfast he was glottal-stopping with the best of them.

He returned to the great bedroom with a well-loaded tray. As he had expected, the Farmwife, dressed and shod, was sitting close beside the bed, her hand lying lightly on her husband's hand. She looked up at Hamid politely but as an intruder: please be quiet, don't interrupt us, make him be well and go away. . . . Hamid had no particular eye for beauty in women, perhaps having seen beauty too often at too short a distance, where it dissolves; but he responded to a woman's health, to the firm sweet flesh, the quiver and vigor of full life. And she was fully alive. She was as tender and powerful as a red-deer doe, as unconsciously splendid. He wondered if there were fawns, and then saw the child standing behind her chair. The room, its shutters closed, was all shadow, with a spatter and dappling of broken light across the islands of heavy furniture, the footboard of the bed, the folds of the coverlet, the child's face and dark eyes.

"Hamid-dem," the Farmwife said—despite her absorption in her husband she had caught his name, then, with the desperate keen hearing of the sickroom, where every word carries hope or doom—"I still cannot see him breathe."

"Lay your ear against his chest," he said, in a tone deliberately louder than her whisper. "You'll hear the heart beat, and feel the lungs expand. Though slowly, as I said. Dema, I brought this for you. Now you'll sit here, see, at this table. A little more light, a shutter open, so. It won't disturb him, not at all. Light is good. You are to sit here and eat breakfast. Along with your daughter, who must be hungry too."

She introduced the child, Idi, a girl of five or six, who clapped her hand on her heart and whispered "Give-you-good-day-dema" all in one glottal-stopped word before she shrank back behind her mother.

It is pleasant to be a physician and be obeyed, Hamid reflected, as the Farmwife and her child, large and little images of each other in their shirts and full trousers and silken braided hair, sat at the table where he had put the tray down and meekly ate the breakfast he had brought. He was charmed to see that between them they left not a crumb.

When Makali rose her face had lost the knotted look and her dark eyes, though still large and still concerned, were tranquil. She has a peaceful heart, he thought. At the same moment his physician's eye caught the signs: she was pregnant, probably about three months along. She whispered to the child, who trotted away. She came back to the chair at the bedside, which he had already relinquished.

"I am going to examine and dress his wound," Hamid said. "Will you watch, dema, or come back?"

"Watch," she said.

"Good," he said. Taking off his coat, he asked her to have hot water sent in from the kitchen.

"We have it piped," she said, and went to a door in the farthest shadowy corner. He had not expected such an amenity. Yet he knew that some of these island farms were very ancient places of civilisation, drawing for their comfort and provision on inexhaustible sun, wind, and tide, settled in a way of life as immemorial as that of their plowlands and pastures, as full and secure. Not the show-wealth of the city, but the deep richness of the land, was in the steaming pitcher she brought him, and in the woman who brought it.

"You don't need it boiling?" she asked, and he said, "This is what I want."

She was quick and steady, relieved to have a duty, to be of use. When he bared the great sword-wound across her husband's abdomen he glanced up at her to see how she took it. Compressed lips, a steady gaze.

"This," he said, his fingers above the long, dark, unhealed gash, "looks the worst; but this, here, is the worst. That is superficial, a mere slash as the sword withdrew. But here, it went in, and deep." He probed the wound. There was no shrinking or quiver in the man's body; he lay insensible. "The sword withdrew," Hamid went on, "as the swordsman died. Your husband killed him even as he struck. And took the sword from him. When his men came around him he was holding it in his left hand and his own sword in his right, though he could not rise from his knees. . . . Both those swords came here with us. . . . There, you see? That was a deep thrust. And a wide blade. That was nearly a deathblow. But not quite, not quite. Though to be sure, it took its toll."

He looked up at her openly, hoping she would meet his eyes, hoping to receive from her the glance of acceptance, intelligence, recognition that he had seen in this face and that among Sandry's people. But her eyes were on the purple and livid wound, and her face was simply intent.

"Was it wise to move him, carry him so far?" she asked, not questioning his judgment, but in wonder.

"The Doctor said it would do him no harm," Hamid said. "And it has done none. The fever is gone, as it has been for nine days now." She nodded, for she had felt how cool Farre's skin was. "The inflammation of the wound is if anything less than it was two days ago. The pulse and breath are strong and steady. This was the place for him to be, dema."

"Yes," she said. "Thank you. Thank you, Hamid-dem." Her clear eyes looked into his for a moment before returning to the wound, the motionless, muscular body, the silent face, the closed eyelids.

Surely, Hamid thought, surely if it were true she'd know it! She couldn't have married the man not knowing! But she says nothing. So it's not true, it's only a story. . . . But this thought, which gave him a tremendous relief for a moment, gave way to another: She knows and is hiding from the knowledge. Shutting the shadow into the locked room. Closing her ears in case the word is spoken.

He found he had taken a deep breath and was holding it.

He wished the Farmwife were older, tougher, that she loved her farmer less. He wished he knew what the truth was, and that he need not be the one to speak it.

But on an utterly unexpected impulse, he spoke: "It is not death," he said, very low, almost pleading.

She merely nodded, watching. When he reached for a clean cloth, she had it ready to his hand.

As a physician, he asked her of her pregnancy. She was well, all was well. He ordered her to walk daily, to be two hours out of the sickroom in the open air. He wished he might go with her, for he liked her and it would have been a pleasure to walk beside her, watching her go along tall and lithe and robust. But if she was to leave Farre's side for two hours, he was to replace her there: that was simply understood. He obeyed her implicit orders as she obeyed his explicit ones.

His own freedom was considerable, for she spent most of the day in the sickroom, and there was no use his being there too, little use his being there at all, in fact. Farre needed nothing from him or her or anyone, aside from the little nourishment he took. Twice a day, with infinite patience, she contrived to feed him ten or a dozen sips of Dr. Saker's rich brew of meat and herbs and medicines, which Hamid concocted and strained daily in the kitchen with the cooks' interested aid. Aside from those two halfhours, and once a day the bed jar for a few drops of urine, there was nothing to be done. No chafing or sores developed on Farre's skin. He lay moveless, showing no discomfort. His eyes never opened. Once or twice, she said, in the night, he had moved a little, shuddered. Hamid had not seen him make any movement for days.

Surely, if there was any truth in the old book Dr. Saker had shown him and in Pask's unwilling and enigmatic hints of confirmation, Makali would know? But she said never a word, and it was too late now for him to ask. He had lost his chance. And if he could not speak to her, he would not go behind her back, asking the others if there was any truth in this tale.

Of course there isn't, he told his conscience. A myth, a rumor, a folktale of the "Old Islanders" . . . and the word of an ignorant man, a saddler. . . . Superstition! What do I see when I look at my patient? A deep coma. A deep, restorative coma. Unusual, yes, but not abnormal, not uncanny. Perhaps such a coma, a very long vegetative period of recovery, common to these islanders, an inbred people, would be the origin of the myth, much exaggerated, made fanciful. . . .

They were a healthy lot, and though he offered his services he had little to do once he had reset a boy's badly splinted arm and scraped out an old fellow's leg abscesses. Sometimes little Idi tagged after him. Clearly she adored her father and missed his company. She never asked, "Will he get well," but Hamid had seen her crouched at the bedside, quite still, her cheek against Farre's unresponding hand. Touched by the child's dignity, Hamid asked her what games she and her father had played. She thought a long time before she said, "He would tell me what he was doing and sometimes I could help." Evidently she had simply followed Farre in his daily round of farmwork and management. Hamid provided only an unsatisfactory, frivolous substitute. She would listen to his tales of the court and city for a while, not very interested, and soon would run off to her own small, serious duties.

Hamid grew restive under the burden of being useless.

He found walking soothed him, and went almost daily on a favorite circuit: down to the quay first, and along the dunes to the southeast end of the island, from which he first saw the open sea, free at last of the whispering green levels of the reedbeds. Then up the steepest slope on Sandry, a low hill of worn granite and sparse earth, for the view of sea and tidal dams, island fields and green marshes, from its summit, where a cluster of windmills caught the sea-wind with slender vanes. Then down the slope past the trees, the Old Grove, to the farmhouse. There were a couple of dozen houses in sight from Sandry Hill, but "the farmhouse" was the only one so called, as its owner was called the Husbandman, or Farmer Sandry, or simply Sandry if he was away from the island. And nothing would keep an Islander away from his island but his duty to the crown. Rooted folk, Hamid thought wryly, standing in the lane near the Old Grove to look at the trees.

Elsewhere on the island, indeed on all the islands, there were no trees to speak of. Scrub willows down along the streams, a few orchards of wind-dwarfed, straggling apples. But here in the Grove were great trees, some with mighty trunks, surely hundreds of years old, and none of them less than eight or ten times a man's height. They did not crowd together but grew widely spaced, each spreading its limbs and crown broadly. In the spacious aisles under them grew a few shrubs and ferns and a thin, soft, pleasant grass. Their shade was beautiful on these hot summer days when the sun glared off the sea and the channels and the sea wind scarcely stirred the fiery air. But Hamid did not go under the trees. He stood in the lane, looking at that shade under the heavy foliage.

Not far from the lane he could see in the Grove a sunny gap where an old tree had come down, perishing in a winter gale, maybe a century ago, for nothing was left of the fallen trunk but a grassy hummock a few yards long. No sapling had sprung up or been planted to replace the old tree; only a wild rose, rejoicing in the light, flowered thornily over the ruin of its stump.

Hamid walked on, gazing ahead at the house he now knew so well, the massive slate roofs, the shuttered window of the room where Makali was sitting now beside her husband, waiting for him to wake.

"Makali, Makali," he said under his breath, grieving for her, angry with her, angry with himself, sorry for himself, listening to the sound of her name.

The room was dark to his still sun-bedazzled eyes, but he went to his patient with a certain decisiveness, almost abruptness, and turned back the sheet. He palpated, ausculted, took the pulse.

"His breathing has been harsh," Makali murmured.

"He's dehydrated. Needs water."

She rose to fetch the little silver bowl and spoon she used to feed him his soup and water, but Hamid shook his head. The picture in Dr. Saker's ancient book was vivid in his mind, a woodcut, showing exactly what must be done—what must be done, that is, if one believed this myth, which he did not, nor did Makali, or she would surely have said something by now! And yet, there was nothing else to be done. Farre's face was sunken, his hair came loose at a touch. He was dying, very slowly, of thirst.

"The bed must be tipped, so that his head is high, his feet low," Hamid said authoritatively. "The easiest way will be to take off the footboard. Tebra will give me a hand." She went out and returned with the yardman, Tebra, and with him Hamid briskly set about the business. They got the bed fixed at such a slant that he put a webbing strap round Farre's chest to keep him from sliding quite down. He asked Makali for a waterproof sheet or cape. Then, fetching a deep copper basin from the kitchen, he filled it with cold water. He spread the sheet of oilskin she had brought under Farre's legs and feet, and propped the basin in an overturned footstool so that it held steady as he laid Farre's feet in the water.

"It must be kept full enough that his soles touch the water," he said to Makali.

"It will keep him cool," she said, asking, uncertain. Hamid did not answer.

Her troubled, frightened look enraged him. He left the room without saying more.

When he returned in the evening she said, "His breathing is much easier."

No doubt, Hamid thought, ausculting, now that he breathes once a minute.

"Hamid-dem," she said, "there is . . . something I noticed. . . ."

"Yes."

She heard his ironic, hostile tone, as he did. Both winced. But she was started, had begun to speak, could only go on.

"His . . ." She started again. "It seemed . . ." She drew the sheet down farther, exposing Harre's genitals.

The penis lay almost indistinguishable from the testicles and the brown, grained skin of the inner groin, as if it had sunk into them, as if all were returning to an indistinguishable unity, a featureless solidity.

"Yes," Hamid said, expressionless, shocked in spite of himself. "The . . . the process is following . . . what is said to be its course."

She looked at him across her husband's body. "But—Can't you—?"

He stood silent awhile. "It seems that—My information is that in these cases—a very grave shock to the system, to the body"—he paused, trying to find words—"such as an injury or a great loss, a grief—but in this case, an injury, an almost fatal wound—a wound that almost certainly would have been fatal, had not it inaugurated the . . . the process in question, the inherited capacity . . . propensity . . ."

She stood still, still gazing straight at him, so that all the big words shrank to nothing in his mouth. He stooped and with his deft, professional gentleness opened Farre's closed eyelid. "Look!" he said.

She too stooped to look, to see the blind eye exposed, without pupil, iris, or white, a polished, featureless, brown bead.

When her indrawn breath was repeated and again repeated in a dragging sob, Hamid burst out at last, "But you knew, surely! You knew when you married him."

"Knew," said her dreadful indrawn voice.

The hair stood up on Hamid's arms and scalp. He could not look at her. He lowered the eyelid, thin and stiff as a dry leaf.

She turned away and walked slowly across the long room into the shadows.

"They laugh about it," said the deep, dry voice he had never heard, out of the shadows. "On the land, in the city, people laugh about it, don't they. They talk about the wooden men, the block-heads, the Old Islanders. They don't laugh about it, here. When he married me—" She turned to face Hamid, stepping into the shaft of warm twilight from the one unshuttered window so that her clothing glimmered white. "When Farre of Sandry, Farre Older, courted me and married me, on the Broad Isle where I lived, the people there said *don't do it* to me, and the people here said *don't do it* to him. Marry your own kind, marry in your own kind. But what did we care for that? He didn't care and I didn't care. I didn't believe! I wouldn't believe! But I came here—Those trees, the Grove, the older trees—you've been there, you've seen them. Do you know they have names?" She stopped, and the dragging, gasping, indrawn sob began again. She took hold of a chairback and stood racking it back and forth. "He took me there. 'That is my grandfather,'" she said in a hoarse, jeering gasp. "'That's Aita, my mother's grandmother. Doran-dem has stood four hundred years.'"

Her voice failed.

"We don't laugh about it," Hamid said. "It is a tale—something that might be true—a mystery. Who they are, the . . . the olders, what makes them change . . . how it happens . . . Dr. Saker sent me here not only to be of use but to learn. To verify . . . the process."

"The process," Makali said.

She came back to the bedside, facing him across it, across the stiff body, the log in the bed.

"What am I carrying here?" she asked, soft and hoarse, her hands on her belly.

"A child," Hamid said, without hesitating and clearly.

"What kind of child?"

"Does it matter?"

She said nothing.

"His child, your child, as your daughter is. Do you know what kind of child Idi is?"

After a while Makali said softly, "Like me. She does not have the amber eyes."

"Would you care less for her if she did?"

"No," she said.

She stood silent. She looked down at her husband, then toward the windows, then straight at Hamid.

"You came to learn," she said.

"Yes. And to give what help I can give."

She nodded. "Thank you," she said.

He laid his hand a moment on his heart.

She sat down in her usual place beside the bed with a deep, very quiet breath, too quiet to be a sigh.

Hamid opened his mouth. "He's blind, deaf, without feeling. He doesn't know if you're there or not there. He's a log, a block, you need not keep this vigil!" All these words said themselves aloud in his mind, but he did not speak one of them. He closed his mouth and stood silent.

"How long?" she asked in her usual soft voice.

"I don't know. That change . . . came quickly. Maybe not long now."

She nodded. She laid her hand on her husband's hand, her light warm touch on the hard bones under hard skin, the long, strong, motionless fingers.

"Once," she said, "he showed me the stump of one of the old-ers, one that fell down a long time ago."

Hamid nodded, thinking of the sunny clearing in the Grove, the wild rose.

"It had broken right across in a great storm, the trunk had been rotten. It was old, ancient, they weren't sure even who . . . the name . . . hundreds of years old. The roots were still in the ground but the trunk was rotten. So it broke right across in the gale. But the stump was still there in the ground. And you could see. He showed me." After a pause she said, "You could see the bones. The leg bones. In the trunk of the tree. Like pieces of ivory. Inside it. Broken off with it." After another silence, she said, "So they do die. Finally."

Hamid nodded.

Silence again. Though he listened and watched almost auto-matically, Hamid did not see Farre's chest rise or fall.

"You may go whenever you like, Hamid-dem," she said gen-tly. "I'm all right now. Thank you."

He went to his room. On the table, under the lamp when he lighted it, lay some leaves. He had picked them up from the bor-der of the lane that went by the Grove, the Grove of the older trees. A few dry leaves, a twig. What their blossom was, their fruit, he did not know. It was summer, between the flower and the seed. And he dared not take a branch, a twig, a leaf from the liv-ing tree.

When he joined the people of the farm for supper, old Pask was there.

"Doctor-dem," the saddler said in his rumbling bass, "is he turning?"

"Yes," Hamid said.

"So you're giving him water?"

"Yes."

"You must give him water, dema," the old man said, relentless. "She doesn't know. She's not his kind. She doesn't know his needs."

"But she bears his seed," said Hamid, grinning suddenly, fiercely, at the old man.

Pask did not smile or make any sign, his stiff face impassive. He said, "Yes. The girl's not, but the other may be older." And he turned away.

Next morning after he had sent Makali out for her walk, Hamid studied Farre's feet. They were extended fully into the water, as if he had stretched downward to it, and the skin looked softer. The long brown toes stretched apart a little. And his hands, still motionless, seemed longer, the fingers knotted as with arthritis yet powerful, lying spread on the coverlet at his sides.

Makali came back ruddy and sweaty from her walk in the summer morning. Her vitality, her vulnerability, were infinitely moving and pathetic to Hamid after his long contemplation of a slow, inexorable toughening, hardening, withdrawal. He said, "Makali-dem, there is no need for you to be here all day. There is nothing to do for him but keep the water basin full."

"So it means nothing to him that I sit by him," she said, half questioning, half stating.

"I think it does not. Not any more."

She nodded.

Her gallantry touched him. He longed to help her. "Dema, did he, did anyone ever speak to you about—if this should happen—There may be ways we can ease the change, things that are traditionally done—I don't know them. Are there people here whom I might ask—Pask and Dyadi—?"

"Oh, they'll know what to do when the time comes," she said, with an edge in her voice. "They'll see to it that it's done right. The right way, the old way. You don't have to worry about that. The doctor doesn't have to bury his patient, after all. The gravediggers do that."

"He is not dead."

"No. Only blind and deaf and dumb and doesn't know if I'm in the room or a hundred miles away." She looked up at Hamid, a gaze which for some reason embarrassed him. "If I stuck a knife in his hand would he feel it?" she asked.

He chose to take the question as one of curiosity, desire to know. "The response to any stimulus has grown steadily less," he said, "and in the last few days it has disappeared. That is, response to any stimulus I've offered." He took up Farre's wrist and pinched it as hard as he could, though the skin was so tough now and the flesh so dry that he had difficulty doing so.

She watched. "He was ticklish," she said.

Hamid shook his head. He touched the sole of the long brown foot that rested in the basin of water; there was no withdrawal, no response at all.

"So he feels nothing. Nothing hurts him," she said.

"I think not."

"Lucky him."

Embarrassed again, Hamid bent down to study the wound. He had left off the bandages, for the slash had closed, leaving a clean seam, and the deep gash had developed a tough lip all round it, a barky ring that was well on the way to sealing it shut.

"I could carve my name on him," Makali said, leaning close to Hamid, and then she bent down over the inert body, kissing and stroking and holding it, her tears running down.

When she had wept awhile, Hamid went to call the women of the household, and they came gathering round her full of solace and took her off to another room. Left alone, Hamid drew the sheet back up over Farre's chest; he felt a satisfaction in her having wept at last, having broken down. Tears were the natural reaction, and the necessary one. A woman clears her mind by weeping, a woman had told him once.

He flicked his thumbnail hard against Farre's shoulder. It was like flicking the headboard, the night table—his nail stung for a moment. He felt a surge of anger against his patient, no patient, no man at all, not any more.

Was his own mind clear? What was he angry with Farre for?

Could the man help being what he was, or what he was becoming?

Hamid went out of the house and walked his circuit, went to his own room to read. Late in the afternoon he went to the sickroom. No one was there with Farre. He pulled out the chair she had sat in so many days and nights and sat down. The shadowy silence of the room soothed his mind. A healing was occurring here: a strange healing, a mystery, frightening, but real. Farre had travelled from mortal injury and pain to this quietness; had turned from death to this different, this other life, this older life. Was there any wrong in that? Only that he wronged her in leaving her behind, and he must have done that, and more cruelly, if he had died.

Or was the cruelty in his not dying?

Hamid was still there pondering, half asleep in the twilit serenity of the room, when Makali came in quietly and lighted a dim lamp. She wore a loose, light shirt that showed the movement of her full breasts, and her gauze trousers were gathered at the ankle above her bare feet; it was a hot night, sultry, the air stagnant on the salt marshes and the sandy fields of the island. She came around the bedstead. Hamid started to get up.

"No, no, stay. I'm sorry, Hamid-dem. Forgive me. Don't get up. I only wanted to apologise for behaving like a child."

"Grief must find its way out," he said.

"I hate to cry. Tears empty me. And pregnancy makes one cry over nothing."

"This is a grief worth crying for, dema."

"Oh, yes," she said. "If we had loved each other. Then I might have cried that basin full." She spoke with a hard lightness. "But that was over years ago. He went off to the war to get away from me. This child I carry, it isn't his. He was always cold, always slow. Always what he is now."

She looked down at the figure in the bed with a quick, strange, challenging glance.

"They were right," she said. "Half alive shouldn't marry the living. If your wife was a stick, was a stump, a lump of wood, wouldn't you seek some friend of flesh and blood? Wouldn't you seek the love of your own kind?"

As she spoke she came nearer to Hamid, very near, stooping over him. Her closeness, the movement of her clothing, the warmth and smell of her body, filled his world suddenly and entirely, and when she laid her hands on his shoulders he reached up to her, sinking upward into her, pulling her down onto him to drink her body with his mouth, to impale her heavy softness on the aching point of his desire, so lost in her that she had pulled away from him before he knew it. She was turning from him, turning to the bed, where with a long, creaking groan the stiff body trembled and shook, trying to bend, to rise, and the round blank balls of the eyes stared out under lifted eyelids.

"There!" Makali cried, breaking free of Hamid's hold, standing triumphant. "Farre!"

The stiff half-lifted arms, the outspread fingers, trembled like branches in the wind. No more than that. Again the deep, cracking, creaking groan from within the rigid body. She huddled up against it on the tilted bed, stroking the face and kissing the unblinking eyes, the lips, the breast, the scarred belly, the lump between the joined, grown-together legs. "Go back now," she murmured, "go back to sleep. Go back, my dear, my own, my love, go back now, now I know, now I know. . . ."

Hamid broke from his paralysis and left the room, the house, striding blindly out into the luminous midsummer night. He was very angry with her, for using him; presently with himself, for being usable. His outrage began to die away as he walked. Stopping, seeing where he was, he gave a short, rueful, startled laugh. He had gone astray off the lane, following a path that led right into the Old Grove, a path he had never taken before.

All around him, near and far, the huge trunks of the trees were almost invisible under the massive darkness of their crowns.

Here and there the moonlight struck through the foliage, making the edges of the leaves silver, pooling like quicksilver in the grass. It was cool under the older trees, windless, perfectly silent.

Hamid shivered.

"He'll be with you soon," he said to the thick-bodied, huge-armed, deep-rooted, dark presences. "Pask and the others know what to do. He'll be here soon. And she'll come here with the baby, summer afternoons, and sit in his shade. Maybe she'll be buried here. At his roots. But I am not staying here." He was walking as he spoke, back towards the farmhouse and the quay and the channels through the reeds and the roads that led inland, north, away. "If you don't mind, I'm on my way, right away. . . ."

The olders stood unmoved as he hurried out from under them and strode down the lane, a dwindling figure, too slight, too quick to be noticed.

THE WISE WOMAN

I came to the place where that woman lived, and I didn't like it at all. It was desolate. It smelled of bones.

She had a house with dead windows. Nobody moved outside or in, but there was a sound like voices inside the house, voices talking all the time. I listened but couldn't understand a word when I listened, could scarcely even hear the voices. When I stopped listening I heard them again, talking and talking.

The ground all round outside the house was stony and bare.

I didn't want to go in. I didn't want to knock at that door. I didn't want to be in that place.

It was near night when I got there, so I decided to knock on the door in the morning. I put my pack down near some bushes just over the hill from the house, unrolled my sleeping bag, ate a little although I wasn't hungry, and slept badly. There were no stars.

In the morning I woke up and thought, I'm not going in there! And I washed my face cheerfully and drank at the boggy stream in the hollow, and set back off over the hills the way I'd come, singing to pace my stride.

But my songs didn't last, and the green hills I'd come through the day before looked brown and dry. Around noon I sat down for a while to ease my shoulders, sore and stiff with the weight of my pack. When I got up I turned back. I went back to the place. I came in sight of the house at sunset. I went no nearer.

I hung around there for days, living on the little food I had, not being hungry, drinking at the boggy stream. I tried once to leave again. I went a whole day's journey that time, but that night I lay sleepless all night, desolate, in despair. I got up in the first grey of dawn and all day walked back to that house.

It was early evening when I got there. I went across the stony yard to the door and knocked on it with my hand. All the voices the house was full of went still. I stood in terror and misery in that silence.

"Come in," she said.

I had to push the door open. I had to go in. I held my breath because the smell of bones caught in my throat, tightening it like a band. I went in.

"Sit down," that woman said.

She sat by her cold hearth. I did not want to sit on the backless stool by her dead fire, but I sat down on it, across the hearth from her.

"Nothing to offer you," she said, without apology. I was glad of it, for my throat was still closed, and my breath came short, so that I could not have eaten or drunk.

"So," she said.

I drew my breath as best I could. "I need your help," I said.

"My help? But you're the Wise Woman," she said, without irony.

"So they call me."

She repeated, still without irony, "So they call you."

In all the voice I could make come out of my throat I said, "I don't know what to do with them."

"Ah," she said. And after a while she said, "Show me."

I reached my lame arms round and took off my pack. I

opened it and took out all my dead, one by one, the long mother, the step mother, the grand father, the hard father, the heavy, heavy baby, the broken friends, and the bad meat of my love. I laid them on the hearthstones, there where there was no fire in the ashes. That woman looked at them. She clicked her tongue. "You wise folk," she said. "What burdens you do carry! I don't know how you can stand up."

"I can't," I said. It is true. My back is bent over, hunched, and my head pushed forward by the weight of what I have carried so long and far.

"Are they on your back when you sleep?" she asked.

I shook my head.

"Where are they, then?"

"On my breast, in my arms."

She clicked her tongue again, and shook her head, as if in imitation of me.

"Aunty," I said. "Please help me!"

She looked carefully at my dead. Though she did not touch them, she got up to walk around them, bending down to peer at the baby, to sniff at the rotten meat, to gaze a long time at the heap of broken friends.

"Why ever didn't you bury them!" she said at last, not reproachful, but amazed.

"I didn't know how. Teach me, please, teach me how. I can't go on carrying them!"

"I should think not," that woman said, and cawed like a crow. She hopped across my dead on the hearthstones, holding out her long black arms. "I can't teach you, Wise Woman. What do you want? To be rid of them? To give them to me? Is that what you want?"

I stood on one side of the hearth and she on the other and my dead lay between us.

"No," I said. I picked the dead up one by one and put them back into my pack, my heavy burden that has bowed my spine and flattened my breasts and made my bones ache. But when I put the pack on my shoulders, it weighed no more than a crow's feather.

"What price wisdom now?" that woman said, sitting by her fireless hearth, without irony, without apology, without reproach.

So I kissed her and went on my way home.

THE POACHER

... And must one kiss
Revoke the silent house, the birdsong wilderness?
                                    —*Sylvia Townsend Warner*

I was a child when I came to the great hedge for the first time. I
was hunting mushrooms, not for sport, as I have read ladies and
gentlemen do, but in earnest. To hunt without need is the privilege, they say, of noblemen. I should say that it is one of the acts
that makes a man a nobleman, that constitutes privilege itself. To
hunt because one is hungry is the lot of the commoner. All it generally makes of him is a poacher. I was poaching mushrooms,
then, in the King's Forest.

My father had sent me out that morning with a basket and
the command, "Don't come sneaking back here till it's full!" I
knew he would beat me if I didn't come back with the basket full
of something to eat—mushrooms at best, at this time of year, or
the fiddleheads of ferns that were just beginning to poke through
the cold ground in a few places. He would hit me across the
shoulders with the hoe handle or a switch, and send me to bed
supperless, because he was hungry and disappointed. He could

feel that he was at least better off than somebody, if he made me hungrier than himself, and sore and ashamed as well. After a while my stepmother would pass silently by my corner of the hut and leave on my pallet or in my hand some scrap she had contrived or saved from her own scant supper—half a crust, a lump of pease pudding. Her eyes told me eloquently, Don't say anything! I said nothing. I never thanked her. I ate the food in darkness.

Often my father would beat her. It was my fate, fortunate or misfortunate, not to feel better off than her when I saw her beaten. Instead I felt more ashamed than ever, worse off even than the weeping, wretched woman. She could do nothing, and I could do nothing for her. Once I tried to sweep out the hut when she was working in our field, so that things would be in order when she came back, but my sweeping only stirred the dirt around. When she came in from hoeing, filthy and weary, she noticed nothing, but set straight to building up the fire, fetching water, and so on, while my father, as filthy and weary as she, sat down in the one chair we had with a great sigh. And I was angry because I had, after all, done nothing at all.

I remembered that when my father first married her, when I was quite small, she had played with me like another child. She knew knife-toss games, and taught me them. She taught me the ABC from a book she had. The nuns had brought her up, and she knew her letters, poor thing. My father had a notion that I might be let into the friary if I learned to read, and make the family rich. That came to nothing, of course. She was little and weak and not the help to him at work my mother had been, and things did not prosper for us. My lessons in reading ended soon.

It was she who found I was a clever hunter and taught me what to look for—the golden and brown mushrooms, woodmasters and morels and other fungi, the wild shoots, roots, berries, and hips in their seasons, the cresses in the streams; she taught me to make fishtraps; my father showed me how to set snares for rabbits. They soon came to count on me for a good portion of our food, for everything we grew on our field went to the Baron, who owned it, and we were allowed to cultivate only a mere patch of kitchen garden, lest our labors there detract from our work for the Baron. I took pride in my foraging, and went willingly into the forest, and fearlessly. Did we not live on the very edge of the forest, almost in it? Did I not know every path and glade and grove within a mile of our hut? I thought of it as my own domain. But my father still ordered me to go, every morning, as if I needed his command, and he laced it with distrust—"Don't come sneaking back until the basket's full!"

That was no easy matter sometimes—in early spring, when nothing was up yet—like the day I first saw the great hedge. Old snow still lay greyish in the shadows of the oaks. I went on, finding not a mushroom nor a fiddlehead. Mummied berries hung on the brambles, tasting of decay. There had been no fish in the trap, no rabbit in the snares, and the crayfish were still hiding in the mud. I went on farther than I had yet gone, hoping to discover a new fernbrake, or trace a squirrel's nut-hoard by her tracks on the glazed and porous snow. I was trudging along easily enough, having found a path almost as good as a road, like the avenue that led to the Baron's hall. Cold sunlight lay between the tall beechtrees that stood along it. At the end of it was something like a hedgerow, but high, so high I had taken it at first for clouds. Was it the end of the forest? the end of the world?

I stared as I walked, but never stopped walking. The nearer I came the more amazing it was—a hedge taller than the ancient beeches, and stretching as far as I could see to left and right. Like any hedgerow, it was made of shrubs and trees that laced and wove themselves together as they grew, but they were immensely tall, and thick, and thorny. At this time of the year the branches were black and bare, but nowhere could I find the least gap or hole to let me peer through to the other side. From the huge roots up, the thorns were impenetrably tangled. I pressed my face up close, and got well scratched for my pains, but saw nothing but an endless dark tangle of gnarled stems and fierce branches.

Well, I thought, if they're brambles, at least I've found a lot of berries, come summer!—for I didn't think about much but food, when I was a child. It was my whole business and chief interest.

All the same, a child's mind will wander. Sometimes when I'd had enough to eat for supper, I'd lie watching our tiny hearthfire dying down, and wonder what was on the other side of the great hedge of thorns.

The hedge was indeed a treasury of berries and haws, so that I was often there all summer and autumn. It took me half the morning to get there, but when the great hedge was bearing, I could fill my basket and sack with berries or haws in no time at all, and then I had all the middle of the day to spend as I pleased, alone. Oftenest what pleased me was to wander along beside the hedge, eating a particularly fine blackberry here and there, dreaming formless dreams. I knew no tales then, except the terribly simple one of my father, my stepmother, and myself, and so my daydreams had no shape or story to them. But all the time I walked, I had half an eye for any kind of gap or opening that might be a way through the hedge. If I had a story to tell myself, that was it: There is a way through the great hedge, and I discover it.

Climbing it was out of the question. It was the tallest thing I had ever seen, and all up that great height the thorns of the branches were as long as my fingers and sharp as sewing needles. If I was careless picking berries from it, my clothes got caught and ripped, and my arms were a net of red and black scratches every summer.

Yet I liked to go there, and to walk beside it. One day of early summer, some years after I first found the hedge, I went there. It was too soon for berries, but when the thorns blossomed the flowered sprays rose up and up one above the other like clouds into the sky, and I liked to see that, and to smell their scent, as heavy as the smell of meat or bread, but sweet. I set off to the right. The walking was easy, all along the hedge, as if there might have been a road there once. The sun-dappling arms of the old beeches of the forest did not quite reach to the thorny wall that bore its highest sprays of blossom high above their crowns. It was shady under the wall, smelling heavily of blackberry flowers, and windlessly hot. It was always very silent there, a silence that came through the hedge.

I had noticed long ago that I never heard a bird sing on the other side, though their spring songs might be ringing down every aisle of the forest. Sometimes I saw birds fly over the hedge, but I never was sure I saw the same one fly back.

So I wandered on in the silence, on the springy grass, keeping an eye out for the little russet-brown mushrooms that were my favorites, when I began to feel something queer about the grass and the woods and the flowering hedge. I thought I had never walked this far before, and yet it all looked as if I had seen it many times. Surely I knew that clump of young birches, one bent down by last winter's long snow? Then I saw, not far from the birches, under a currant bush beside the grassy way, a basket and a knotted sack. Someone else was here, where I had never met another soul. Someone was poaching in my domain.

People in the village feared the forest. Because our hut was almost under the trees of the forest, people feared us. I never understood what they were afraid of. They talked about wolves. I had seen a wolf's track once, and sometimes heard the lonely voices, winter nights, but no wolf came near the houses or fields. People talked about bears. Nobody in our village had ever seen a bear or a bear's track. People talked about dangers in the forest, perils and enchantments, and rolled their eyes and whispered, and I thought them all great fools. I knew nothing of enchantments. I went to and fro in the forest and up and down in it as if it were my kitchen garden, and never yet had I found anything to fear.

So whenever I had to go the half-mile from our hut and enter the village, people looked askance at me, and called me the wild boy. And I took pride in being called wild. I might have been happier if they had smiled at me and called me by my name, but as it was, I had my pride, my domain, my wilderness, where no one but I dared go.

So it was with fear and pain that I gazed at the signs of an intruder, an interloper, a rival—until I recognised the bag and basket as my own. I had walked right round the great hedge. It was a circle. My forest was all outside it. The other side of it was—whatever it was—inside.

From that afternoon, my lazy curiosity about the great hedge grew to a desire and resolve to penetrate it and see for myself that hidden place within, that secret. Lying watching the dying embers at night, I thought now about the tools I would need to cut through the hedge, and how I could get such tools. The poor little hoes and mattocks we worked our field with would scarcely scratch those great stems and branches. I needed a real blade, and a good stone to whet it on.

So began my career as a thief.

An old woodcutter down in the village died; I heard of his death at market that day. I knew he had lived alone, and was called a miser. He might have what I needed. That night when my father and stepmother slept, I crept out of the hut and went back by moonlight to the village. The door of the cottage was open. A fire smoldered in the hearth under the smokehole. In the sleeping end of the house, to the left of the fire, a couple of women had laid out the corpse. They were sitting up by it, chatting, now and then putting up a howl or two of keening when they thought about it. I went softly in to the stall end of the cottage; the fire was between us, and they did not see or hear me. The cow chewed her cud, the cat watched me, the women across the fire mumbled and laughed, and the old man lay stark on his pallet in his winding-sheet. I looked through his tools, quietly, but without hurrying. He had a fine hatchet, a crude saw, and a mounted, circular grindstone—a treasure to me. I could not take the mounting, but stuck the handle in my shirt, took the tools under my arm and the stone in both hands, and walked out again. "Who's there?" said one of the women, without interest, and sent up a perfunctory wail.

The stone all but pulled my arms out before I got it up the road to our hut, where I hid it and the tools and the handle a little way inside the forest under a bit of brushwood. I crept back into the windowless blackness of the hut and felt my way over to my pallet, for the fire was dead. I lay a long time, my heart beating hard, telling my story: I had stolen my weapons, now I would lay my siege on the great thorn hedge. But I did not use those words. I knew nothing of sieges, wars, victories, all such matters of great history. I knew no story but my own.

It would be a very dull one to read in a book. I cannot tell much of it. All that summer and autumn, winter and spring, and the next summer, and the next autumn, and the next winter, I fought my war, I laid my siege: I chopped and hewed and hacked at the thicket of bramble and thorn. I cut through a thick, tough trunk, but could not pull it free till I had cut through fifty branches tangled in its branches. When it was free I dragged it out and then I began to cut at the next thick trunk. My hatchet grew dull a thousand times. I had made a mount for the grind-stone, and on it I sharpened the hatchet a thousand times, till the blade was worn down into the thickness of the metal and would not hold an edge. In the first winter, the saw shivered against a rootstock hard as flint. In the second summer, I stole an ax and a handsaw from a party of travelling woodcutters camped a little way inside the forest near the road to the Baron's hall. They were poaching wood from my domain, the forest. In return, I poached tools from them. I felt it was a fair trade.

My father grumbled at my long absences, but I kept up my foraging, and had so many snares out that we had rabbit as often as we wanted it. In any case, he no longer dared strike me. I was sixteen or seventeen years old, I suppose, and though I was by no means well grown, or tall, or very strong, I was stronger than he, a worn-out old man, forty years old or more. He struck my stepmother as often as he liked. She was a little, toothless, red-eyed, old woman now. She spoke very seldom. When she spoke my father would cuff her, railing at women's chatter, women's nagging. "Will you never be quiet?" he would shout, and she would shrink away, drawing her head down in her hunched shoulders like a turtle. And yet sometimes when she washed herself at night with a rag and a basin of water warmed in the ashes, her blanket would slip down, and I saw her body was fine-skinned, with soft breasts and rounded hips shadowy in the firelight. I would turn away, for she was frightened and ashamed when she saw me looking at her. She called me "son," though I was not her son. Long ago she had called me by my name.

Once I saw her watching me as I ate. It had been a good harvest, that first autumn, and we had turnips right through the winter. She watched me with a look on her face, and I knew she wanted to ask me then, while my father was out of the house, what it was I did all day in the forest, why my shirt and vest and trousers were forever ripped and shredded, why my hands were callused on the palms and crosshatched with a thousand scratches on the backs. If she had asked I would have told her. But she did not ask. She turned her face down into the shadows, silent.

Shadows and silence filled the passage I had hacked into the great hedge. The thorn trees stood so tall and thickly branched above it that no light at all made its way down through them.

As the first year came round, I had hacked and sawn and chopped a passage of about my height and twice my length into the hedge. It was as impenetrable as ever before me, not allowing a glimpse of what might be on the other side nor a hint that the tangle of branches might be any thinner. Many a time at night I lay hearing my father snore and said to myself that when I was an old man like him, I would cut through the last branch and come out into the forest—having spent my life tunnelling through nothing but a great, round bramble patch, with nothing inside it but itself. I told that end to my story, but did not believe it. I tried to tell other ends. I said, I will find a green lawn inside the hedge . . . A village . . . A friary . . . A hall . . . A stony field . . . I knew nothing else that one might find. But these endings did not hold my mind for long; soon I was thinking again of how I should cut the next thick trunk that stood in my way. My story was the story of cutting a way through an endless thicket of thorny branches, and nothing more. And to tell it would take as long as it took to do it.

On a day near the end of winter, such a day as makes it seem there will never be an end to winter, a chill, damp, dark, dreary, hungry day, I was sawing away with the woodcutters' saw at a gnarled, knotted whitethorn as thick as my thigh and hard as iron. I crouched in the small space I had and sawed away with nothing in my mind but sawing.

The hedge grew unnaturally fast, in season and out; even in midwinter thick, pale shoots would grow across my passageway, and in summer I had to spend some time every day clearing out new growth, thorny green sprays full of stinging sap. My passage or tunnel was now more than five yards long, but only a foot and a half high except at the very end; I had learned to wriggle in, and keep the passage man-high only at the end, where I must have room enough to get a purchase on my ax or saw. I crouched at my work, glad to give up the comfort of standing for a gain in going forward.

The whitethorn trunk split suddenly, in the contrary, evil way the trees of that thicket had. It sent the sawblade almost across my thigh, and as the tree fell against others interlaced with it, a long branch whipped across my face. Thorns raked my eyelids and forehead. Blinded with blood, I thought it had struck my eyes. I knelt, wiping away the blood with hands that trembled from strain and the suddenness of the accident. I got one eye clear at last, and then the other, and, blinking and peering, saw light before me.

The whitethorn in falling had left a gap, and in the maze and crisscross of dark branches beyond it was a small clear space, through which one could see, as through a chink in a wall: and in that small bright space I saw the castle.

I know now what to call it. What I saw then I had no name for. I saw sunlight on a yellow stone wall. Looking closer, I saw a door in the wall. Beside the door stood figures, men perhaps, in shadow, unmoving; after a time I thought they were figures carved in stone, such as I had seen at the doors of the friary church. I could see nothing else: sunlight, bright stone, the door, the shadowy figures. Everywhere else the branches and trunks and dead leaves of the hedge massed before me as they had for two years, impenetrably dark.

I thought, if I was a snake I could crawl through that hole! But being no snake, I set to work to enlarge it. My hands still shook, but I took the ax and struck and struck at the massed and crossing branches. Now I knew which branch to cut, which stem to chop: whichever lay between my eyes and that golden wall, that door. I cared nothing for the height or width of my passage, so long as I could force and tear my way forward, indifferent to the laceration of my arms and face and clothing. I swung my dull ax with such violence that the branches flew before me; and as I pushed forward the branches and stems of the hedge grew thinner, weaker. Light shone through them. From winter-black and hard they became green and soft, as I hacked and forced on forward, until I could put them aside with my hand. I parted the last screen and crawled on hands and knees out onto a lawn of bright grass.

Overhead the sky was the soft blue of early summer. Before me, a little downhill from the hedge, stood the house of yellow stone, the castle, in its moat. Flags hung motionless from its pointed towers. The air was still and warm. Nothing moved.

I crouched there, as motionless as everything else, except for my breath, which came loud and hard for a long time. Beside my sweaty, blood-streaked hand a little bee sat on a clover blossom, not stirring, honey-drunk.

I raised myself to my knees and looked all round me, cautious. I knew that this must be a hall, like the Baron's hall above the village, and therefore dangerous to anyone who did not live there or have work there. It was much larger and finer than the Baron's hall, and infinitely fairer; larger and fairer even than the friary church. With its yellow walls and red roofs it looked, I thought, like a flower. I had not seen much else I could compare it to. The Baron's hall was a squat keep with a scumble of huts and barns about it; the church was grey and grim, the carved figures by its door faceless with age. This house, whatever it was, was delicate and fine and fresh. The sunlight on it made me think of the firelight on my stepmother's breasts.

Halfway down the wide, grassy slope to the moat, a few cows lay in midday torpor, heads up, eyes closed; they were not even chewing the cud. On the farther slope, a flock of sheep lay scattered out, and an apple orchard was just losing its last blossoms.

The air was very warm. In my torn, ragged shirt and coat, I would have been shivering as the sweat cooled on me, on the other side of the hedge, where winter was. Here I shrugged off the coat. The blood from all my scratches, drying, made my skin draw and itch, so that I began to look with longing at the water in the moat. Blue and glassy it lay, very tempting. I was thirsty, too. My waterbottle lay back in the passage, nearly empty. I thought of it, but never turned my head to look back.

No one had moved, on the lawns or in the gardens around the house or on the bridge across the moat, all the time I had been kneeling here in the shadow of the great hedge, gazing my fill. The cows lay like stones, though now and again I saw a brown flank shudder off a fly, or the very tip of a tail twitch lazily. When I looked down I saw the little bee still on the clover blossom. I touched its wing curiously, wondering if it was dead. Its feelers shivered a little, but it did not stir. I looked back at the house, at the windows, and at the door—a side door—which I had first seen through the branches. I saw, without for some while knowing that I saw, that the two carved figures by the door were living men. They stood one on each side of the door as if in readiness for someone entering from the garden or the stables; one held a staff, the other a pike; and they were both leaning right back against the wall, sound asleep.

It did not surprise me. They're asleep, I thought. It seemed natural enough, here. I think I knew even then where I had come.

I do not mean that I knew the story, as you may know it. I did not know why they were asleep, how it had come about that they were asleep. I did not know the beginning of their story, nor the end. I did not know who was in the castle. But I knew already that they were all asleep. It was very strange, and I thought I should be afraid; but I could not feel any fear.

So even then, as I stood up, and went slowly down the sunny sward to the willows by the moat, I walked, not as if I were in a dream, but as if I were a dream. I didn't know who was dreaming me, if not myself, but it didn't matter. I knelt in the shade of the willows and put my sore hands down into the cool water of the moat. Just beyond my reach a golden-speckled carp floated, sleeping. A waterskater poised motionless on four tiny dimples in the skin of the water. Under the bridge, a swallow and her nestlings slept in their mud nest. A window was open, up in the castle wall; I saw a silky dark head pillowed on a pudgy arm on the window ledge.

I stripped, slow and quiet in my dream movements, and slid into the water. Though I could not swim, I had often bathed in shallow streams in the forest. The moat was deep, but I clung to the stone coping; presently I found a willow root that reached out from the stones, where I could sit with only my head out, and watch the golden-speckled carp hang in the clear, shadowed water.

I climbed out at last, refreshed and clean. I rinsed out my sweaty, winter-foul shirt and trousers, scrubbing them with stones, and spread them to dry in the hot sun on the grass above the willows. I had left my coat and my thick, straw-stuffed clogs up under the hedge. When my shirt and trousers were half dry I put them on—deliciously cool and wet-smelling—and combed my hair with my fingers. Then I stood up and walked to the end of the drawbridge.

I crossed it, always going slowly and quietly, without fear or hurry.

The old porter sat by the great door of the castle, his chin right down on his chest. He snored long, soft snores.

I pushed at the tall, iron-studded, oaken door. It opened with a little groan. Two boarhounds sprawled on the flagstone floor just inside, huge dogs, sound asleep. One of them "hunted" in his sleep, scrabbling his big legs, and then lay still again. The air inside the castle was still and shadowy, as the air outside was still and bright. There was no sound, inside or out. No bird sang, or woman; no voice spoke, or foot stirred, or bell struck the hour. The cooks slept over their cauldrons in the kitchen, the maids slept at their dusting and their mending, the king and his grooms slept by the sleeping horses in the stableyard, and the queen at her embroidery frame slept among her women. The cat slept by the mousehole, and the mice between the walls. The moth slept on the woollens, and the music slept in the strings of the minstrel's harp. There were no hours. The sun slept in the blue sky, and the shadows of the willows on the water never moved.

I know, I know it was not my enchantment. I had broken, hacked, chopped, forced my way into it. I know I am a poacher. I never learned how to be anything else. Even my forest, my domain as I had thought it, was never mine. It was the King's Forest, and the king slept here in his castle in the heart of his forest. But it had been a long time since anyone talked of the king. Petty barons held sway all round the forest; woodcutters stole wood from it, peasant boys snared rabbits in it; stray princes rode through it now and then, perhaps, hunting the red deer, not even knowing they were trespassing.

I knew I trespassed, but I could not see the harm. I did, of course, eat their food. The venison pastry that the chief cook had just taken out of the oven smelled so delicious that hungry flesh could not endure it. I arranged the chief cook in a more comfortable position on the slate floor of the kitchen, with his hat crumpled up for a pillow; and then I attacked the great pie, breaking off a corner with my hands and cramming it in my mouth. It was still warm, savoury, succulent. I ate my fill. Next time I came through the kitchen, the pastry was whole, unbroken. The enchantment held. Was it that as a dream, I could change nothing of this deep reality of sleep? I ate as I pleased, and always the cauldron of soup was full again and the loaves waited in the pantry, their brown crusts unbroken. The red wine brimmed the crystal goblet by the seneschal's hand, however many times I raised it, saluted him in thanks, and drank.

As I explored the castle and its grounds and outbuildings—always unhurriedly, wandering from room to room, pausing often, often lingering over some painted scene or fantastic tapestry or piece of fine workmanship in tool or fitting or furniture, often settling down on a soft, curtained bed or a sunny, grassy garden nook to sleep (for there was no night here, and I slept when I was tired and woke when I was refreshed)—as I wandered through all the rooms and offices and cellars and halls and barns and servants' quarters, I came to know, almost as if they were furniture too, the people who slept here and there, leaning or sitting or lying down, however they had chanced to be when the enchantment stole upon them and their eyes grew heavy, their breathing quiet, their limbs lax and still. A shepherd up on the hill had been pissing into a gopher's hole; he had settled down in a heap and slept contentedly, as no doubt the gopher was doing down in the dirt. The chief cook, as I have said, lay as if struck down unwilling in the heat of his art, and though I tried many times to pillow his head and arrange his limbs more comfortably, he always frowned, as if to say, "Don't bother me now, I'm busy!" Up at the top of the old apple orchard lay a couple of lovers, peasants like me. He, his rough trousers pulled down, lay as he had slid off her, face buried in the blossom-littered grass, drowned in sleep and satisfaction. She, a short, buxom young woman with apple-red cheeks and nipples, lay sprawled right out, skirts hiked to her waist, legs parted and arms wide, smiling in her sleep. It was again more than hungry flesh could endure. I laid myself down softly on her, kissing those red nipples, and came into her honey sweetness. She smiled in her sleep again, whenever I did so, and sometimes made a little groaning grunt of pleasure. Afterwards I would lie beside her, a partner to her friend on the other side, and drowse, and wake to see the unfalling late blossoms on the apple boughs. When I slept, there inside the great hedge, I never dreamed.

What had I to dream of? Surely I had all I could desire. Still, while the time passed that did not pass, used as I was to solitude, I grew lonely; the company of the sleepers grew wearisome to me. Mild and harmless as they were, and dear as many of them became to me as I lived among them, they were no better companions to me than a child's wooden toys, to which he must lend his own voice and soul. I sought work, not only to repay them for their food and beds, but because I was, after all, used to working. I polished the silver, I swept and reswept the floors where the dust lay so still, I groomed all the sleeping horses, I arranged the books on the shelves. And that led me to open a book, in mere idleness, and puzzle at the words in it.

I had not had a book in my hands since that primer of my stepmother's, nor seen any other but the priest's book in the church when we went to Mass at Yuletime. At first I looked only at the pictures, which were marvelous, and entertained me much. But I began to want to know what the words said about the pictures. When I came to study the shapes of the letters, they began to come back to me: *a* like a cat sitting, and the fatbellied *b* and *d*, and *t* the carpenter's square, and so on. And a-t was at, and c-a-t was cat, and so on. And time enough to learn to read, time enough and more than enough, slow as I might be. So I came to read, first the romances and histories in the queen's rooms, where I first had begun to read, and then the king's library of books about wars and kingdoms and travels and famous men, and finally the princess's books of fairy tales. So it is that I know now what a castle is, and a king, and a seneschal, and a story, and so can write my own.

But I was never happy going into the tower room, where the fairy tales were. I went there the first time; after the first time, I went there only for the books in the shelf beside the door. I would take a book, looking only at the shelf, and go away again at once, down the winding stair. I never looked at her but once, the first time, the one time.

She was alone in her room. She sat near the window, in a little straight chair. The thread she had been spinning lay across her lap and trailed to the floor. The thread was white; her dress was white and green. The spindle lay in her open hand. It had pricked her thumb, and the point of it still stuck just above the little thumb-joint. Her hands were small and delicate. She was younger even than I when I came there, hardly more than a child, and had never done any hard work at all. You could see that. She slept more sweetly than any of them, even the maid with the pudgy arm and the silky hair, even the rosy baby in the cradle in the gatekeeper's house, even the grandmother in the little south room, whom I loved best of all. I used to talk to the grandmother, when I was lonely. She sat so quietly as if looking out the window, and it was easy to believe that she was listening to me and only thinking before she answered.

But the princess's sleep was sweeter even than that. It was like a butterfly's sleep.

I knew, I knew as soon as I entered her room, that first time, that one time, as soon as I saw her I knew that she, she alone in all the castle, might wake at any moment. I knew that she, alone of all of them, all of us, was dreaming. I knew that if I spoke in that tower room she would hear me: maybe not waken, but hear me in her sleep, and her dreams would change. I knew that if I touched her or even came close to her I would trouble her dreams. If I so much as touched that spindle, moved it so that it did not pierce her thumb—and I longed to do that, for it was painful to see— but if I did that, if I moved the spindle, a drop of red blood would well up slowly on the delicate little cushion of flesh above the joint. And her eyes would open. Her eyes would open slowly; she would look at me. And the enchantment would be broken, the dream at an end.

I have lived here within the great hedge till I am older than my father ever was. I am as old as the grandmother in the south room, grey-haired. I have not climbed the winding stair for many years. I do not read the books of fairy tales any longer, nor visit the sweet orchard. I sit in the garden in the sunshine. When the prince comes riding, and strikes his way clear through the hedge of thorns—my two years' toil—with one blow of his privileged, bright sword, when he strides up the winding stair to the tower room, when he stoops to kiss her, and the spindle falls from her hand, and the drop of blood wells like a tiny ruby on the white skin, when she opens her eyes slowly and yawns, she will look up at him. As the castle begins to stir, the petals to fall, the little bee to move and buzz on the clover blossom, she will look up at him through the mists and tag-ends of dream, a hundred years of dreams; and I wonder if, for a moment, she will think, "Is that the face I dreamed of seeing?" But by then I will be out by the midden heap, sleeping sounder than they ever did.